public
ENEMY #1

public ENEMY #1

KIKI SWINSON

www.kensingtonbooks.com

DAFINA BOOKS are published by

Kensington Publishing Corp.
119 West 40th Street
New York, NY 10018

All Kensington Titles, Imprints, and Distributed Lines are available at special quantity discounts for bulk purchases for sales promotions, premiums, fundraising, and educational or institutional use. Special book excerpts or customized printings can also be created to fit specific needs. For details, write or phone the office of the Kensington special sales manager: Kensington Publishing Corp., 119 West 40th Street, New York, NY 10018, attn: Special Sales Department, Phone: 1-800-221-2647.

Library of Congress Card Catalogue Number: 2020952373

The DAFINA logo is a trademark of Kensington Publishing Corp.

ISBN-13: 978-1-4967-2976-7
ISBN-10: 1-4967-2976-5
First Kensington Hardcover Edition: May 2021

ISBN-13: 978-1-4967-2979-8 (ebook)
ISBN-10: 1-4967-2979-X (ebook)

10 9 8 7 6 5 4 3 2 1

Printed in the United States of America

public
ENEMY #1

1

KHLOÉ

I was hesitant to meet this woman, Frances Larson, until she promised to pay me forty thousand dollars to look into her husband's suicide. I couldn't believe it—only a day after resigning from the news media, I walked into the opportunity of a lifetime. I knew I had the skills to pull off the job Frances wanted me to do, but I also knew that I'd have to be smarter about the moves I made this time around.

When Frances and I spoke over the phone, I had her meet me at the Starbucks so I could see her in person and get a feel for who I'd be working for. As soon as Frances walked into the Starbucks café, I instantly knew that she was the one I was waiting to meet. She wore all black, as she said she would. Her body language was noticeable and I could see the confidence in her eyes. She looked like she ruled the world.

As she approached me, our eyes connected and that's when I stood up on my feet. After she got within arm's reach of me, we extended our hands at the same time and gave each other the proper handshake. "How are you?" I asked her. I was mesmerized by her beauty. She and the singer Rihanna looked almost identical.

"I'm great. Thank you for asking," she replied, and then she took a seat in the chair next to me.

"I see that you're carrying a bundle of joy."

She cracked a smile. "Yes, I am. Some days are good and some are bad, which is why I need to handle this situation I'm in so I can move on with my life."

"That's understandable. So, what can I do for you?" I got straight to the point.

"I want you to investigate my late husband's death. His fellow police officers are saying that he killed himself, but I know my husband, and committing suicide is something I know he wouldn't do. He was a Christian man and Christians don't kill themselves," she protested.

"What do you think happened?" I wondered aloud.

"I believe he was murdered by the other narcotics detectives in his unit."

"And why would the cops in his unit want to kill him?"

"Because he was about to blow the whistle on a cover-up within the precinct."

"Those are some very heavy allegations," I told her.

"What I am telling you are facts. And the sooner you start your investigation on those cop killers, the sooner you'll discover the cops in this town are not protecting and serving the people of our city, they're killing them off and leaving them dead in the streets."

"Can you provide me with the names of your husband's colleagues?"

"They're on a piece of paper inside of this envelope. Their home addresses and the model and year of their cars are listed underneath their names. I even put pictures of those bastards in here too," she replied and pushed a medium-size manila envelope across the table towards me.

I grabbed the envelope and attempted to open it, but she stopped me. "No, please don't open that here. Someone could be watching us. Wait until you get alone and do it," she instructed me.

Alarmed by Frances's behavior and paranoia, I couldn't help but look around at everyone sitting in Starbucks. Once I scanned my surrounding area, I peered out of the glass window near our table.

"Stop looking around at everyone. You're gonna bring attention to us," Frances demanded, but it was barely above a whisper.

"I'm sorry. But I can't help it. Do you see how paranoid you're acting?" I pointed out.

"Never mind all of that, let's just stick to the script," she said nonchalantly, but in a way to silence me and curtail my behavior so she could continue to control this meeting. "There are four names in that envelope. And those names belong to some very powerful narcotics detectives in this city. What I want you to do is find out as much dirt on them as you can. Dirt that could get them put away in prison for the rest of their lives. I don't even want their spouses to get their pension. I want them erased from the face of this earth for what they did to my husband. That whole squad are supposed to get honored for a huge drug bust they did a couple weeks ago. So, I want them exposed before that honor ceremony."

"When is that ceremony?"

"In five days."

"Oh no, that's impossible, especially for what you want me to do."

"I will pay you whatever you want," she offered. It was evident that money was no object to her. Dollars and money signs started circling around in my head. "Come on, Khloé, I know you can do it. Just name your price."

But I was mum. I hadn't done this type of work before, so I didn't know what to charge her. "What are you willing to pay for this job?" I questioned her just to get a feel of what dollar amount she was willing to pay. "And before you answer, keep in mind what you're hiring me to do. I mean, this thing could get extremely ugly. And perhaps deadly," I expressed.

"I know that, and that's why I told you to name your price," she agreed.

I sat there for another couple seconds trying to figure out what would be a good price to charge this chick. I didn't know what kind of money she was working with. For all I knew, she could be living off her husband's pension and insurance policy payout. And boom, that's when it hit me that she was probably gonna pay me with his insurance policy. And that policy could be worth a couple hundred thousand dollars. With his insurance policy payout, social security money and pension, she could be sitting on half a million dollars. "Pay me fifty K and I'll start working on this today," I blurted out, knowing in my heart that she was going to tell me hell no. I waited for her answer.

"I'll pay you forty thousand," she countered me.

"Deal." I agreed without hesitating. Unbeknownst to her, I would've taken ten thousand dollars if she had offered it. Fortunately for me, I threw the fishing bait in the water and she bit.

"There's five thousand dollars cash in that envelope. So, how would you like for me to pay you the balance?"

"Wire it to my bank?"

"Who do you bank with?" she asked me as she pulled her cell phone from her handbag.

"Wells Fargo," I told her.

"Awesome, I bank there too," she said while logging in to her browser and clicking on the link to the Wells Fargo website. After she logged into her account, she asked me for my account number. And just like that, after a few clicks, Frances had wired the balance of thirty-five thousand dollars into my bank account. "There, it's done," she assured me as she flashed the confirmation number and the amount of the transfer before my eyes.

I smiled at her and said, "Let the games begin."

2

THE TIME STARTS NOW—KHLOÉ

While I watched Frances leave Starbucks ahead of me, my mind shifted to my deadline to dig up dirt on those pigs that killed her husband. Realizing this was nearly impossible to do, and the fact that it could become deadly, I knew that I was going to need some muscle. And the only man I trusted to do that was my uncle Eddie Mercer. He was an OG from the streets, so I knew that I would be in good hands.

As soon as I got in my car, I grabbed my cell phone from my front pocket and dialed my uncle's cell phone number. While I waited for him to answer, I opened the envelope and looked at the photos of the cops that I had to investigate. I knew all of them. Not personally, but I'd heard stories. Some good and some bad.

"Hello," I heard my uncle Eddie say.

"Hey, Uncle Eddie, got a minute?" I asked him as I sifted through photos I had before me.

"Sure, baby girl. What's up?" His voice was a deep baritone. Uncle Eddie is my late mother's brother. He's the oldest of my grandmother's three children and he made sure everyone that walked into my grandmother's house knew it. He was the black sheep. As a child, I watched my uncle Eddie terrorize people through the years. His Suge Knight resemblance and posture made people fearful of him. His continuous bouts with law enforcement always made him a target, which was why he'd spent twenty-five of his forty-four years in prison. From the day he joined the Ace of Spades gang back in the late eighties, he made no secret of it. He wore their color bandanas and black T-shirts like a badge of honor. Word on the streets was he'd caught over ten bodies since he first joined the gang. But the cops could only prove that he murdered one. As of this moment, I know that he's still a member but he's not active. At least, that's what he told me.

"I've got a job for you if you want it," I started off.

"You fucking right, I want it. What do I have to do?"

"I don't wanna talk about it over the phone, so let's get together within the next hour and I'll answer all your questions then," I explained.

"Where are you now?" he wanted to know.

"I'm just now leaving the Starbuck's down on Colley Ave."

"Meet me at Maggie's apartment. I'll be here waiting on you."

"Okay, I'm on my way to you right now," I assured him and then I ended the call. After I placed my cell phone in the cup holder, I shoved the photos of the cops back in the envelope. But before pulling my hand out of the envelope, I grabbed the money that was inside. It was five thousand dollars, like Frances had said it was. Having this money in my hand and the other thirty-five thousand in my bank account gave me courage and optimism that I could conquer anything that came my way. Armed with those two things, I shoved the money down in my purse and then I powered up the ignition so I could get this show on the road.

As I drove away from Starbucks, I caught a quick glimpse

of Frances as she drove right by me in the opposite direction in her late model, soccer mom, E-Class Mercedes station wagon. Instead of blowing her car horn at me, she gave me a head nod. It was a nod of confidence. She had the look of a spoiled, rich man's wife who got what she wanted without getting her nails dirty in the process. But that wasn't her story. I could tell that Frances was a ride-or-die chick. And she'd do whatever it took to get the answers she wanted, no matter the cost.

The drive to my uncle's girlfriend's house was a hop and a jump from where I was currently. Her name was Maggie Ashe. She lived in an income-based housing complex off Little Creek Road and Hampton Boulevard. It was walking distance to the Norfolk Naval Station. The apartment complex has been around for as long as I could remember. That ought to give anyone a sense of its condition and the outside landscaping.

When I pulled into the parking lot of this five-duplex community, I was greeted by a dozen bad-ass kids running around unsupervised while a bunch of young thugs between the ages of fourteen and eighteen shared two blunts as they amused themselves with conversation and laughter. Everyone in this clique looked just alike. I swear, you couldn't tell them apart because they all wore dreadlocks. It was a sight for sore eyes.

While I listened to two of the guys go head-to-head in a battle rap, I texted Uncle Eddie and told him that I was outside. Thankfully, he didn't make me wait long. He came out of Maggie's apartment a few seconds later. "What's up, chief," I heard one of the young guys say.

"What's good, OG?" I heard another young guy say. The other guys gave my uncle the proper handshake.

After seeing this, there was no question in my mind that my uncle was very respected by the old and the young and that he was going to be the perfect man for the job I had for him.

"Hey, beautiful," he said with a huge smile after he climbed into the passenger seat and closed the door behind himself.

I smiled back. "Hey, Uncle Ed!"

He leaned in towards me, gave me a kiss, and then he rested his back against the seat. "Whatcha got for me?" he wanted to know. He was truly eager to hear what I had to say. He had no idea that I was as eager as he was. I mean, he and I never really had a relationship, with all his trips back and forth to prison. I guess this was a nice trade-off, from my dad, Kyle, to him. I don't think he ever got over the fact my dad took a bullet for him doing a home invasion back when I was just a toddler. He reminds me of this more times than I can count.

"I know you heard that I quit the TV station, right?"

"Yeah, I heard something like that."

"Well, now I'm doing private investigative work and I just got my first client, so I'm gonna need your help."

"Private eye, huh?"

"Yes," I said as confidently as I could.

"What kind of help do you need from me?"

"I'm gonna need your protection."

"From who?"

"Everybody. You know that if my twin, Kyle, was alive, he'd be my right hand."

"You're right. But how come it sounds like there's more that you're not telling me?"

"Look, Unc, my client was married to a narc cop . . . and—" I said, but was cut off in midsentence.

"Oh nah, baby girl. I ain't getting involved with that," he said adamantly.

"But wait, Unc. Let me finish," I begged him.

"Go ahead," he encouraged me, but his facial expression sent a different message.

I cleared my throat and said, "Did you hear about a narc cop that supposedly committed suicide not too long ago?"

"I heard about it."

"Well, the lady that hired me was married to that cop. And here are photos of the other cops that he was working with." I pulled the pictures from the manila envelope and showed them to him.

"You know that he was a dirty cop, right?"

"That's what I've been told."

"So, if you know this, then why are you getting involved with that? Nobody liked that cop. Plenty of dudes wanted that nigga dead, even those other cop buddies you got pictures of wanted his head on the platter, that's why when they killed him, they made it look like he did it himself."

"Listen, Uncle Eddie, I understand all of that. But that lady offered me a nice piece of change to get her some answers, so I've gotta help her."

"Khloé, you're gonna put yourself in a dangerous situation."

"It couldn't be any worse than that murder case I reported a few weeks ago."

Uncle Eddie turned away from me and stared out the passenger-side window at the young guys standing not too far from where I was parked.

"Come on, Uncle Ed, I need you. It's not gonna be as bad as you think. During the daytime I'm gonna beat the street alone, but when it gets dark and I don't feel comfortable going somewhere by myself, that's when I'm gonna need your assistance."

Once again, he didn't reply. He kept his attention on the boys outside my car.

"Tell you what, I will give you six thousand dollars, and all you have to do is watch my back. Okay?"

The mention of money got his attention and he turned back around and faced me. "I'll do it, but when we're out together, I'm gonna tell you when and where to go. Got it?"

I smiled. "Got it!" I said, and then I gave him a big kiss on his cheek.

"When am I gonna get my six grand?" he didn't hesitate to ask me.

"Tell you what, here's three thousand now." I reached into my purse and took out thirty one-hundred-dollar bills. "I'll give you the other three thousand when the job is done."

"Got it," he replied, taking the money from my hands. "What are you about to get into now?"

"I'm going home so I can gather my thoughts. I gotta figure out how I'm going to handle this case."

"A'ight, well, call me later after you figure things out."

"Will do," I assured him, while I leaned in to kiss him on the left cheek.

"Drive safe, baby girl," he replied and then he got out of my car.

I watched him as he walked away. But before he could make his way up the flight of stairs that led to his girlfriend's apartment, I turned my car in the opposite direction and exited the parking area of this duplex.

"Thank you, Jesus!" I said as I drove away. Knowing that my uncle was going to protect me while I worked this case made me feel overjoyed. Nothing could stop me now.

3

PROTECTION MODE—UNCLE EDDIE

Maggie was sitting on the living room sofa when I walked back in the apartment. She gave me a half smile while she watched my facial expression and body language. She and I had been together for a couple of years now, so she knew my mannerisms to a tee. Maggie was an attractive woman. Everybody told her she looked like Mary J. Blige, but I didn't see the resemblance. She looked more like Angela Bassett to me. But regardless of who she looked like, she was a good woman and she was a good mother to her son. Jamie was twenty. He was an active member in the same gang. He was a soldier too. He had so much heart that you couldn't deny him respect. If you did, then he'd take it from you. That's just how that dude rolled.

"So, what were you and Khloé talking about?" she asked me. Under normal circumstances I would not lie to Maggie. But this was some other level type of shit and I felt like the conversation I just had with my niece needed to stay between us.

"She was just stopping by to tell me thanks for having her back after all that other shit went down with that murder," I lied.

"She better keep her ass off the streets. These streets are grimy, Ed, and there's word going around about her being a snitch."

"She's not a snitch. She was only doing her job. And as long as I'm alive, no harm will come to her. Trust me, she's gonna be all right," I tried to assure her, and then I headed into the kitchen.

"God forbid, but what if something happens to you?" She threw another question at me as she got up from the sofa and followed me into the kitchen.

"Come on now, you know my peoples ain't gonna let anything happen to her. They already know that if something does happen to me, then they're gonna step up and protect her," I replied while getting a bottle of Corona beer from the refrigerator. By this time, Maggie was within arm's distance of me.

After I closed the fridge, I turned around and faced her. She said, "Just be careful. I wouldn't know what to do if I couldn't have you in my life anymore."

I leaned in and kissed her on her forehead. "I've got everything under control," I told her, and then I removed the bottle cap from my beer and took in a mouthful.

Instead of hanging around in the kitchen, I walked back into the living room and sat back down on the sofa. Maggie flopped down on the sofa next to me. "What's that bulging through your pants pocket?" she wanted to know as she eyed my front left-side pants pocket.

I knew the answer to her question without looking down at my pants pocket, but I did it anyway. This was my way of prolonging the inevitable. Or maybe it was my way of playing mind games.

"Your pockets weren't looking like that before you left out of this apartment." She pressed the issue.

I looked up from my pants and smiled at her after taking

another gulp of beer. She instantly punched me playfully in my arm. "Is that money?" she asked me. She wouldn't let up.

"Yes, it is," I finally responded after taking another sip of beer.

She started patting my pockets. "How much is it?"

I set the bottle of Corona down on the coffee table in front of me, and then I stuck my hand down in my pocket and pulled out all the money. Maggie's eyes doubled in size and then she snatched all the money from my left hand. "How much is this?"

"It's three grand."

"Oh my God, Eddie, did Khloé give this to you?" she wondered aloud. On one hand, she sounded excited that she had a stack of money in her hand, but then her body language gave off a different vibe. She looked a bit nervous and concerned. "Did you get this from Khloé?" She pressed the issue . . .

"Yeah, she lent it to me. I told her that I wanted to get you a new living room furniture set. You know, fix up the place," I lied. This was the quickest story that I could come up with in this short amount of time.

"And where did she get this kind of money from? They don't pay news reporters a lot of money, especially in the Tidewater area."

My lies continued. "She said that she got it from her savings." I changed the subject. "So, whatcha wanna do? Get new living room furniture? Or a new bedroom set?"

"Maybe we should fix things up in the living room first," she suggested.

"Okay, let's do it," I encouraged her. My goal was to give her what she wanted and keep a smile on her face. She was my princess. My ride-or-die, and as long as she holds me down, I would do the same.

"I'm gonna put this money away before someone walks in here without knocking first," she stated as she stood up.

"I wish someone would walk in here," I said, and then I took another mouthful of beer. Maggie chuckled as she walked away and headed down the hallway to our bedroom. To see her happy made me feel really good inside. I felt like the king in my own castle. And feeling like a king is the best feeling a man could have.

While Maggie was in our bedroom, someone knocked on the front door. "Who is it?" I yelled from the sofa.

"It's me, Lily," a woman's voice yelled back from the other side of the door.

"Come in," I continued.

It only took two seconds for my front door to open and when it did, my next-door neighbor Lily appeared. Lily Freeman was a twenty-nine-year-old hoe, with three kids all under the age of ten, and they were all by different dudes. She wasn't a bad-looking girl, she was just so ratchet. With the right amount of makeup on her face, she could pass for one of those reality chicks you see on *Love & Hip Hop: Atlanta*. I'm talking lace-front weaves and ass shots. But unfortunately for her, she couldn't hook up with a cat with a little dough in his pockets. All the dudes she fucked with, either stole cars or robbed other dope boys around the city. Let's just say the pickings for a decent dude were slim to nothing. They just don't make brothers like me anymore. So she's gonna either have to relocate to the "A" or find herself a hustle that'll put some serious cash in her pockets.

"Is Maggie here?" she asked after she stepped inside.

"Maggie, Lily's here!" I yelled to the back of the apartment.

"I'm coming," Maggie yelled back. Seconds later, I heard Maggie's footsteps coming our way.

"What's up, girl?" Maggie asked Lily after coming within three feet of her.

"I'm making meat loaf for dinner and ran out of ketchup. Think I could get a little bit of yours?" Lily asked her.

"Yeah, sure," Maggie replied, and then they both headed into the kitchen.

Hearing Lily say that she needed to borrow ketchup was a new low for her. The last time she borrowed food was a week ago when she came over and asked Maggie could she borrow four eggs because she wanted to cook for a dude she met the night before. With all the niggas she's got running in and out of her apartment, she should keep food in her crib, especially condiments. All I can do right now is shake my head.

I sat on the sofa and started watching TV while Maggie entertained Lily's goofy ass. Maggie didn't know it, but I fucked Lily a couple of times when Maggie went up to Maryland to see her family. That very day she left, Lily asked me if she could borrow twenty dollars and said she would pay me back the next day. I told her that she wouldn't have to pay me back if she got naked in front of me so I could jerk off. She told me that she could do me one better by giving me some head and let me hit the pussy. And I gotta admit that her pussy ain't that bad. She gave me some mean head too. She sucked my dick better than Maggie did.

That incident happened a month ago. I haven't fucked her since, but I've given her a few dollars here and there for some head. Boy, I can't imagine what would happen if Maggie ever found out about that! But I do know that it would probably be World War III around this bitch.

"So, who are you cooking for?" Maggie wanted to know.

"This new dude I met named Red," Lily gushed.

"What kind of name is Red?" Maggie's questions continued.

"He said his real name was Reggie. But everybody calls him Red."

"And where did you meet him?"

"At the laundromat yesterday."

"And what was he doing at the laundromat?"

"I think he hustles out of there. I saw him sitting in the corner taking money from one of these dope fiends around here, so he probably sells drugs," Lily explained.

"You better be careful, bringing in all these new guys around your kids. He could be a killer for all you know," Maggie warned her.

Lily chuckled. "Girl, ain't nothing gonna happen to me or my kids. Trust me. I've got everything under control."

"I hope you're right. 'Cause if something jumps off, me and Eddie won't be coming down there to get in the middle of your mess."

"We sure ain't," I blurted out.

Maggie and Lily both turned around and looked at me. "Will you mind your business and watch TV please, sir," Maggie joked.

"I was, until I heard my name," I spoke up, and then I turned my attention back towards the television.

Lily stayed over and talked to Maggie for another five minutes about things that only women talk about. I eventually zoned them out. Listening to women's problems isn't what I deem entertaining. I was a type of dude that wanted to make some good money, eat some good food, watch a little bit of sports, have a drama-free life, and some good pussy. That's it. I'm just a simple guy.

4

MAKING A DETOUR—KHLOÉ

I swear, for some reason I hate driving to the service station to get gas for my car. It is such an inconvenience. But this time I had to stop. My fuel light had lit up and I knew that I only had a couple of miles left before my car stalled and I found myself on the side of the road. A local gas station was only half a mile up the street, so that's where I stopped to get gas.

After driving into the parking lot of the station, I pulled up to pump five. I grabbed my debit card from my wallet, hopped out of my car, paid for my gas, and then I put the hose into my tank and started fueling my car. While I waited for the tank to fill up, the doorbell on the gas station's door chimed as it opened, so I looked up and noticed a very familiar face. It was a chick named Farrah Gomez. She and I went to middle school and high school together. In our senior yearbook, she was voted Most Likely to Achieve while I was voted Best Dressed. I felt in my heart that I was supposed to be Most Likely to Achieve, not her. After graduation, I heard that she went off to college at UCLA to pursue a master's degree in Pediatrics medicine. I have not seen her since, so seeing her now felt really weird.

Before I could say anything, she looked up from her purse as she walked in my direction. "Khloé, is that you?" she asked as her eyes grew in size. I could tell that she was truly surprised to see me. I even had to admit that I was surprised to see her as well.

"Yes, it is." I smiled while looking at her from head to toe.

From where I was standing, Farrah hadn't changed one bit. She was the same exact height and weight, and her skin was flawless. She didn't look a day older.

"Girl, you better come over here and give me a hug," she insisted as she walked to the tail end of my car. When we were face-to-face, she extended her arms. I released the gas pump nozzle and extended my arms to hug her back.

"What is that perfume you're wearing? It smells so good," she complimented me after we released one another.

"It's the Prada," I told her. "So, when did you come into town?"

"A week ago. My cousin Taylor got married a couple days ago. So I came here for that. You remember her, right?"

"Yes, of course I remember Taylor. Doesn't she work down at the precinct in Norfolk on Virginia Beach Boulevard as a desk cop?" I asked her.

Farrah chuckled. "Girl, please, she wishes she were a cop. She's just a desk clerk filing reports for the real police. I'm the only one in my family that's doing something worth talking about," she bragged. From childhood Farrah always put herself on a pedestal. To hear her tell it, no one has accomplished more than she has.

"Are you still living in LA?" I asked her. I knew this was the direction she wanted our conversation to go.

"Yep, and I love it too. I'm one of the directors on the board of medicine at the Children's hospital in LA."

"That's great," I said, but I was sure she wanted me to give her more praise than I'd given. I changed the subject. "Married? Have any kids?"

"No children for right now. I'm not married either. My career takes up too much of my time. Maybe in five years, I'll have them both." She chuckled in a giddy kind of way. "So, what about you?"

"Well, I guess I can say no and no too," I replied bashfully.

"So, what's this I hear about you being a TV reporter? Taylor said that you just cracked open a huge murder case. That's awesome." She applauded me, giving me a congratulatory nudge in my arm. Whether she knew it or not, that little punch stung a little.

"Now I don't know about cracking open a case. All I did was report the news," I replied modestly.

"That's not what I heard," she teased, and nudged me in my arm again. It didn't hurt like the last one, but it was close. Thankfully, the gas pump handle clicked, which meant that my car was filled to the max. It was perfect timing. After I took the hose from my gas tank, I put it back in the pump slot and then I expressed how nice it was seeing her, all while making my way towards the driver-side door of my car. "Girl, let me get out of here. I've got so many errands to run," I lied.

"Okay, well, don't let me hold you up. But give me your number so we can keep in touch," she insisted. "Wait, let me get Taylor on the phone for a second. She's not going to believe me if I tell her that I saw you," she added as she pulled out her cell phone and started dialing numbers. I stood there, dreading to talk and reminisce with someone I couldn't care less about. Taylor was cool back in school, but she was also annoying. Always wanted to be seen. She loved when guys used to drool over her. She fucked like half of the football team. And maybe three guys on the basketball team. I swear, that girl's a piece of work; which shocks me that she found a man to marry her.

"Hey, Cuz, you are not going to believe who I'm standing in front of," Farrah said after she put the call on speaker. If Taylor said something crazy about Farrah putting her on the spot by calling her and putting on speaker phone then I would hear it.

"Who?" Taylor replied.

"Khloé."

"Who—news reporter, Khloé?"

"Yep, and I got you on speaker too," Farrah warned her cousin. "She wanted to say hi."

"Oh cool. Hello Khloé."

"Hi. How are you?" Taylor yelled through the phone.

"I'm good. Keeping myself busy. But never mind me, Farrah just told me that you got married. So, congratulations."

"Thank you. I appreciate that," Taylor replied. "It's weird that Farrah ran into you, because I just told her that you were in LA on the red carpet."

"Oh yeah, she mentioned that to me," Farrah agreed.

"So, I hear that you work for the Norfolk police precinct." I shifted the conversation. I just realized that this call couldn't be so bad after all. Taylor worked for the very people I was being paid to investigate, so maybe I could get her to help me without her even knowing it.

"Yes, I do."

"That's good. I heard they have the best pension and insurance package," I said, trying to stroke her ego.

"Let's just say that I'm not the breadwinner in my household. My husband is a city attorney. He thinks he's a big shot, but he's a pushover around here."

"That's freaking awesome."

"Yeah, it's okay. I tell you what, we're having a dinner party tomorrow night with some high officials in the city. So, why don't you stop by and maybe talk to my husband? You know, do a little interview on him for your news station."

"Well . . ." I started off saying, but she interjected.

"No, don't give me any excuses that you can't come. This could be another big story for you, Ms. Celebrity News Anchor," she insisted.

If she only knew that I wasn't a journalist anymore and that I was a private investigator, wanting to use her to get some information on four dirty-ass cops that work for the city. Would she still agree to let me come to an event for her husband? Well, I could not gamble with that possibility. "You twisted my arm, so I will come," I finally agreed. My mission was to get chummy with hopes that I could milk her for all I could get on those crooked-ass boys. I hoped it worked.

"Perfect. So, Farrah will give you my number and address and I'll see you tomorrow night, seven o'clock sharp."

"Cool, see you there," I said.

Immediately after Taylor ended our call, Farrah gave me Taylor's cell phone number and address. She keyed in my cell phone number in her phone. When she was done, she insisted that I give her another hug, so I did and then I got into my car. "I'm going to be in town for another couple of days, so let's do lunch before I leave."

"I would love that," I lied, but said it cheerfully.

"Cool, well then, take care," she said.

"You too," I replied. Without hesitation, I closed the door to my car and started the ignition. When I drove out of the service station parking lot, I watched Farrah as she got into her midsize rental car and drove away, but she went in a different direction. I swear, seeing her after all this time was a bittersweet moment. On one hand, it felt good to see that after all this time she was doing good in her life. But then, seeing her success made me wish that I had left this town when she had. Who knows, maybe I'd be an anchor for one of those big studio syndicated news programs like *E! News* or *Today*. Hopefully, I do well with this private investigator thing, because if I don't, then I'm back in the trenches trying to capture the next big exclusive!

I could not wait to get back home. I had to sit down and come up with a game plan on how to work this case that I just took on. Now I could only hope that things went smoothly, since my uncle Eddie was on my team. And armed with new information that my childhood friend Taylor Neal worked as a desk clerk down at the precinct on Virginia Beach Boulevard in Norfolk was like music to my ears. I figured that if given the opportunity, I could get her to help me out as well. Now, I knew I couldn't go off and start running my mouth to her about what I was hired to do, but I knew I would have to tell her something. Maybe if I offered the right amount of money, that could do the talking for me. I guessed I would find out sooner than later.

En route to my apartment, my cell phone rang and when I looked down at the caller ID and noticed that it was Mrs. Larson calling me, I answered her call immediately. "Hello," I said.

"Hi, Khloé, this is Frances, do you have a minute?" Her voice sounded alarmed.

"Yes, is there something wrong?"

"I know this is a sudden request, but could we meet somewhere?"

"Is everything all right?"

"Are you home?" she wanted to know.

"No, I'm out. But I am heading to my apartment now," I told her.

"Could you please drive by my home?"

Puzzled by her request, I asked her to repeat herself. "Say that again."

"I think some of the cops that my late husband worked with were following me today. And I think that a couple of them are sitting outside my house watching me from one of their cars."

Caught off guard by her statement, I had to take a deep breath and exhale while I collected my thoughts. I was really at a loss for words, so I just sat there with my phone against my ear, navigating my car down the street.

"Khloé, are you still there?"

"Yes, I'm still here," I answered her. "Okay, so you want me to drive by your house and then do what?"

"See if there's cops sitting in their cars watching my house."

"That's it?"

"Yes, that's all I want you to do. But I want to be on the phone with you when you do it."

"So, what are you going to do if I tell you that I see cops sitting outside your house?"

"Nothing. I mean, what am I going to do, call the cops on the cops?"

"Yeah, why not? It's always good to document things. You know, create a paper trail."

"A paper trail doesn't mean anything to the crooked cops that my husband worked with. If they could steal drugs from the evidence room and get away with it, then filing a complaint is a joke in their eyes," she pointed out.

"Do you fear for your life?" I wanted to know. I needed to feel her out and find out what her mindset was.

"No, I'm not afraid, I just want someone else to know what's going on in case something happens to me."

Taken aback by her statement, I said, "Why don't you leave town for a few weeks? Maybe visit some of your family while I work on your husband's case."

"That's what they want me to do. But I refuse to let them chase me out of town. If those assholes had something to do with my husband's murder, then I want to witness their downfall."

"Are you sure about this? Because we could be going down a dark and scary road."

"Were you afraid to go down the road you traveled when you were investigating that murder you just uncovered?"

"At times I was," I admitted.

"But did that stop you?" She pressed me.

"No."

"Then we have nothing else to discuss. Call me back when you get within a mile of my house," she instructed me.

"Where do you live?"

"I'm sorry, I'm in the Lafayette area of Norfolk. And my address is 391 Colonial Avenue."

"Okay, I got it. I'm putting your address in my GPS as we speak. So, I'll call you as soon as I get within a mile of your home," I assured her.

"Thank you," she said and then the phone went dead silent.

Immediately after Frances disconnected our call, I turned my car around and made a detour to drive in the direction of her house. I followed the instructions of my GPS and was within a mile of Frances's home in less than ten minutes. It was dusk, so the streetlights weren't lit yet, but it was dark enough for a couple of cops to hide out in an unmarked car on the side of the street. So as I approached Frances's home, I realized that she lived on a one-way street. There was only one way in and one way out. This made me nervous because I did not want to stick out like a sore thumb. "I'm about to drive down your block now," I informed her after I dialed her number and got her back on the phone.

"Where are you exactly?" she wanted to know.

"I'm passing a white house on my left and a gray-colored vinyl-siding house to my right," I explained.

"If you drive up a little more, my house is on the right side."

"Okay," I said.

"Have you seen any suspicious-looking undercover vehicles since you've got on my block?"

"No, I haven't. Every car I've driven by looks like a regular civilian vehicle and they've all been empty," I told her.

"Are you sure? I mean, because those guys are crafty when it comes to being inconspicuous and hiding in plain sight."

"Well, trust me when I tell you that no one is out here," I assured her. "Speaking of which, I'm driving past your house right now," I informed her.

"I see you," she replied as she stood in the doorway of her front door and waved at me.

I waved back. "Well, I guess my job is done here," I said.

"Before you leave, will you turn around and give my block another look just in case?" she asked me.

"Yes, I can do that," I told her.

"Thank you," she said, and then she ended the call.

Keeping my word, I circled around the block and took another look just to be sure that no one was watching her home. After I made the second trip, I texted her and told her that no one was outside and then I encouraged her to get some rest. She texted me back and thanked me for being in her corner. Seeing those words from that text message meant a lot to me. It made me feel heroic in a sense, knowing that I did something to make her feel safe. I've always been told that there's strength in numbers, so hopefully we could keep this momentum going.

5

GETTING THE WORD OUT— UNCLE EDDIE

I told Maggie that I was going to run out to the corner store and get a Black & Mild cigar and that I would be back in a few minutes, but she knew that I wasn't coming back for at least an hour. But she didn't care. I had just given her three grand to get some new furniture for our house, so in her eyes I could go out and stay as long as I wanted to. When they say *happy wife, happy life*, that shit is true.

I hopped in my black four-door 2010 Cadillac Seville with nineteen-inch rims. This car was my pride and joy. I kept this motherfucker clean and my tires always looked wet and shiny. When motherfuckers saw my car coming, they knew it was me sitting behind the steering wheel because I didn't let no one drive it but me. Maggie wasn't even allowed to drive it and she was my woman. I got her a four-door 2015 Honda Accord, so she was happy and content and so was I.

* * *

I headed out to my stomping grounds in a part of Norfolk called Park Place. My gang, Ace of Spades, operates on Thirty-First and Thirty-Second Streets. I'm a non-active member, but I still occasionally go to gatherings like cookouts, birthday celebrations, and bring in the New Year with my other OGs to express gratitude and love for our brotherhood. Tonight, though, I had to check in with Tommy Boy. Tommy Boy was one of the leaders and became one right after I did my second bid in prison over fifteen years ago. He was a brown-skinned, tall, slim guy with the stature of Snoop Dog. He didn't have long hair, though. He preferred to be bald-headed. He had the shiniest bald head that I've ever seen. People that didn't know him viewed him as a laid-back individual. But he was vicious, and he would not think twice about killing you, if provoked. He was definitely a killer.

When I pulled up to the house he controlled on Thirty-First Street, there was about twenty little dudes standing around on the lawn and sitting on the front porch. At first glance, every cat posting up in front of the house looked like he wasn't a day over twenty. Wearing all black, they looked trained and ready to do whatever Tommy Boy instructed them to do.

After getting out of my car, I walked towards the gang of dudes and they all stopped talking and acknowledged me by nodding their head and saying, "What's up, chief!" I nodded back as I passed them and went inside the house.

Tommy Boy was sitting in the den in the back of the house. It didn't surprise me when I saw him playing *Madden NFL - 20* with Jay, one of the gang members. Jay was Tommy Boy's right hand. I believed he was in his early thirties and he was a rider too. Built like an armored truck, Jay could be mistaken for a linebacker on an NFL team. He was undeniably a solider in anyone's eyes. The funny thing about him was that he hardly ever smiled. My relationship with him was solid.

But he was Tommy Boy's body guard. Anything Tommy Boy instructed Jay to do, it got done. No questions asked.

"What's good?" I said as I fist-bumped Tommy Boy and then did the same to Jay.

Tommy Boy chuckled. "I'm in here kicking this dude's ass in this game," he bragged.

"That's 'cause his ass is cheating," Jay commented.

I chuckled and then I took a seat on the opposite end of a sofa sectional that stretched around the entire room.

"Trying to get in a game with me?" Tommy Boy asked me.

"Nah, I'm good. I ain't gonna be here long."

"It ain't gon' take that long for me to whip your ass!" Tommy Boy commented while he kept his eyes on the TV, navigating the control buttons on the PlayStation game controller.

"I'll take you up on the offer the next time," I said.

"So, what's up? Whatcha wanna talk about?" Tommy Boy did not hesitate to ask.

"You know my niece Khloé quit her job at the news station and decided to do private investigative work."

"Word?" Tommy casually said.

I began to explain. "Yeah, so this broad named Frances hired her to find out who killed her husband. But the lady's husband is that dead narc cop that news people said had committed suicide."

"Come on, bro, you know that ain't no good look for your niece. And besides, fuck that dude! He robbed a lot of my homeboys and dudes that I did not like. So I say, whatever happened to him, he deserved it," Tommy Boy continued, not once taking his eyes off the television.

"I told her that. But check it out, the lady is paying top dollar to find out what happened to that dude, and all my niece wants is for me to watch her back. Make sure nobody does anything to harm her. So, I'm asking you as a brother to have my back if some shit pops off. I'll give you half of the money my niece has offered to pay me," I stated and then I sat back, hoping that Tommy Boy would come on board with me.

I sat there for at least two whole minutes waiting for him to respond. It felt longer though. But finally he spoke. "How much are you talking?" he asked.

"Three grand," I lied.

"So, you're gonna give me half of that?" He wanted clarity.

"Yeah, it's yours."

"You know under any other circumstances I wouldn't take money from you. But you know I hate fucking cops. I wish all of them would die, especially the ones that has made my life a living hell."

"Come on, Tommy, you know I know that."

"Yeah, I know you know that, but sometimes you gotta reassure family that it's all love," Tommy Boy pointed out as he set the game controller down on the coffee table in front of him. He and Jay's game was over, with Tommy Boy coming out on top as the winner.

Jay set his controller down too. He scooted back on the sectional and then he chimed in. "I'm with Tommy when he said that he doesn't want to fuck with that situation because of that dirty-ass cop. But we are family, and if you want us to ride with you for the sake of your niece, then I'm down. Just let us know what you want us to do."

"She hasn't given me the specifics. But as soon as I find out, I'll call for us to have another sit-down and then we can go from there," I suggested.

"In the meantime, I'll get some of those young dudes outside that we just recruited geared up and ready to go as soon as you give us the word," Jay added.

"Sounds good, my dawgs!" I said, and stood up to leave. Before I walked out, I dapped up both Tommy Boy and Jay and then I assured them that I'd be linking up with them the following day.

It felt good leaving the spot knowing that Tommy Boy and Jay agreed to ride with me and Khloé to get that check that that dirty cop's wife was dishing out. I knew now, that things would go smoothly. And if I made a little more than I was telling them, well, it was all good.

6

DOING MY RESEARCH—KHLOÉ

The moment after I stepped into my apartment, I collapsed onto my living room couch, closed my eyes for a couple of minutes, and thought about what was to come for me and this investigation that I'd been hired to do. The one thing that weighed heavily on my mind was that I had to do this job in five days. I must also add that once I started asking questions about those cops, shit was going hit the fan, so I'd better get ready.

When the sun started shining through the window treatments of my living room, I opened my eyes and knew at that moment that I had fallen asleep on the couch. I must've been tired because I didn't get up in the middle of the night to use the bathroom, and I usually did that every night. Realizing this, I got up and headed to the bathroom. I tinkled and then I turned on the shower water. While I allowed the water to get warm, I grabbed my toothbrush and started brushing my teeth. When I stood in the mirror and brushed my teeth, I always used that time to think about what I needed to do that day. Start working on this cop's case was front and center in my mind. But I knew that I had to take a shower and get dressed before I did anything. So immediately after I brushed my teeth, I got undressed and then I climbed into the shower.

I stayed in the shower for at least fifteen minutes. I wanted to stay in there longer, but the streets were calling and I had to be ready to answer. "Come on, Khloé. Chop! Chop! You need to put some pep in your step," I uttered aloud, urging myself to speed things up so that I could gather my things and leave my house.

While I was getting dressed, my cell phone rang. I grabbed it from the top ledge of my dresser drawer and noticed that it was Frances calling me. I knew she was probably just checking in, so I answered and put the call on speaker. "Hello," I said while sitting on the foot of my bed putting on my sneakers.

"Good morning," she replied.

"Good morning," I stated.

"So, are you out and about?" she wanted to know.

"No, but I will be leaving my apartment in about five minutes," I told her.

"What's first on your agenda?" she questioned me.

"I'm going over those right now," I replied while becoming irritated by her overshadowing behavior.

Her questions continued. "Well, will you have a report for me by the end of the day?"

"Is that what you're requiring me to do?" I asked her, but at the same time dreading her answer.

"Yes, I am. Isn't that what private investigators do?" she said nonchalantly. But then it sounded like she was being sarcastic.

"Have you ever hired a private investigator before?" I questioned her.

"Yes, I have."

"Can I ask you why?" I pressed the issue.

"To find out if my husband was cheating on me."

"Was he?"

"No, he wasn't," she replied confidently. But I knew the bitch was lying. Throughout my journalism career, I have interviewed hundreds of people, so I know when someone is lying.

"Was that private investigator good?" My questions continued.

"Yes, he was."

"So then, why didn't you hire him back?"

"Because I didn't think that he would get the results I needed in a timely manner."

"So, you asked him to take your case?"

"No, I didn't."

"Why not?"

"Because I didn't feel like I could trust him. See, you're a black woman with ties to the streets . . ."

"Wait a minute, what makes you think that?" I cut her off in midsentence.

"I did my homework on you. I went on your Facebook page. I saw the pictures of your family members and learned their names. So I was able to do background checks."

I was shocked by her admission. "Are you serious right now?"

"Yes, I am totally serious. But don't look at it in a bad way. I was just doing my due diligence. I couldn't give you all that money without doing my own background report on you."

Seething at her confession, I wanted to tell her to kiss my ass and that I was going to give her the money back. But I had already given my Uncle Eddie three thousand dollars of it. I did not have that kind of money lying around. Now I had no other choice but to suck it up and continue with this job.

"Okay, so I'm about to head out, and when I get back, I'll call you with an update," I told her.

"Sounds great. I look forward to hearing from you," she replied, and then we ended the call.

"Fucking bitch!" I cursed as I stood up from my bed and shoved my cell phone down in my front pocket.

According to the information I got from that list Frances gave me, all four cops that worked with her late husband worked night shift, so I figured that they would be home around this time. The first person on the list was narcotics Detective Brad Ford. From the looks of it, Brad was the sergeant of these guys. Looking at his photo I could see some cockiness in his facial expression. His resemblance to the actor Steven Seagal was spot-on, a hard-ass with the long ponytail and dark sunshades. Brad also had the physical attributes of a former Navy SEAL. He looked very intimidating to say the least.

After putting his address into my GPS, I realized that he lived fifteen miles away, in a middle-class neighborhood in the Pembroke area of Virginia Beach and that it would only take me about twenty minutes to get there.

The drive to this man's home boosted my adrenaline level for some reason. I was beginning to feel like Wonder Woman. Like I could conquer the world. It might have been the pressure Frances put on my back before ending our call. But whatever it was, I knew that I had a job to do and I was going to do it.

The Pembroke neighborhood landscape was average. The VOTE FOR TRUMP AND PENCE front-lawn signs were everywhere. That alone gave me the impression that this community represented a small number of the MAGA population. Keeping that in mind, I knew that I had to be as inconspicuous as possible. I did not want any of this guy's neighbors to see me and then alert him to my presence.

After my GPS alerted me that I was slowly approaching Brad Ford's home address and that it was five hundred feet on my left, I immediately noticed that a car was backing out of the driveway. I looked at the car dead-on, and when the driver put the car in drive and started driving towards me, I immediately realized that it was Brad. "Shit, please don't look at me. Please don't look at me," I mumbled as I scrambled to grab my sunglasses from my purse that was sitting in the front passenger seat. Fortunately for me, I managed to grab my sunglasses and shove them on my face before he had a chance to drive by me. But then when he drove by me, he did not even look my way. He was too distracted by a conversation he was having on his cell phone to look my way. Now, what a relief that was.

Struggling to turn my car around without being noticed by the cop frustrated me for ten seconds, because I could not move my car until after he made a turn onto the next street. But once he did that, I was able to turn my car around and put the pedal to the metal and make my move.

What made me frustrated all over again was that when I arrived at that same corner, I looked to my right and this cop's car was nowhere to be found. "Fuck! Fuck! Fuck! Where did you go?" I panicked. But I knew that he could not be that far away, so I turned right and started making my way down the next street. After driving a few yards, I finally zoomed in on the car about a quarter of a mile down the road. I swear, it gave me a sigh of relief. "There you go, you dirty cop, you," I said, grinding my teeth. Knowing all the bad shit he had done to the guys in this city gave me a bad taste in my mouth. He was a piece of shit and I was going to get all the dirt I could on him before that award ceremony Frances said would be happening in the next four days. He wouldn't be honored on my watch.

I made sure that my car stayed at least five cars behind

Brad Ford to avoid blowing my cover. After following him for seven miles, we ended up in the parking lot of a small lunch café in the Princess Anne area of Virginia Beach. After he parked his car, he got out and a white woman parked in an SUV next to his car got out and greeted him. They met with a ten-second embrace and then they kissed each other on the mouth. I was floored. "This motherfucker is cheating on his wife," I whispered. After they released each other, they held hands as they made their way towards the café. "I gotta get pictures of this," I said as I grabbed my cell phone and held it up, zoomed in and started flicking the photo button. I think I took at least twenty shots. Once they disappeared into the restaurant, I couldn't take any more photos. I was tempted to go inside, but that would've been overkill, so I stayed in my car.

Three minutes into my stakeout I called Uncle Eddie to tell him what I had just witnessed. He did not answer the phone the first time, so I called him back and he picked up. "I was just about to call you back," he said.

"Is this a bad time?" I asked him.

"Nah, I'm good now. I was helping Maggie bring groceries in the house."

I sparked the conversation. "Well, you'll never guess where I am."

"Where?"

"I'm sitting in my car outside a café where that cop Brad Ford just strolled in with his mistress, holding hands."

"I don't give a damn about that cracker. But I'm sure his wife would feel differently," my uncle commented. "How do you know it's his mistress?"

"Because I just followed him from his house. And this is where we ended up. She was waiting on him in the parking lot of this place when he pulled up and got out of his car."

"You followed him from his crib?"

"Yeah."

"You better be careful, baby girl. That cracker don't play fair. If he finds out that you were following him, I know he'll try to hurt you. And I can't let that happen."

"How can I work this case if I stop following him?"

"Look, I understand you got a job to do. All I'm saying is be careful, especially since I'm not with you," he warned me.

"Don't worry, Unc, I got it," I tried assuring him. "Speaking of which, will you be available to accompany me later tonight? I've got some running around to do and I'm gonna need you to ride with me."

"Of course, what time?"

"Between eight and nine o'clock."

"Are you picking me up? Or do you want me to come to you?"

"I'll pick you up."

"A'ight, I'll be ready," he said.

"See you later," I replied and then we ended the call.

7

GOTTA' EXPLAIN MYSELF— UNCLE EDDIE

"Who was that? Khloé?" Maggie asked me while putting groceries away.

"Yeah, that was her," I replied as I began to leave the kitchen. But just because I was walking away from Maggie, that wasn't going to stop her from questioning me.

"Where are you two going later on?" she wanted to know.

Once again, she questioned me about my suddenly hanging around my niece. Now don't get me wrong, I have hung around Khloé before, but for her to come visit me yesterday and then I walk back in the house with three grand in my pocket, Maggie knew something was up, she just didn't know what it was. "She got some shit going on in her life and she needs my guidance," I finally explained. Not all of what I said was a lie, so my conscience was still intact as far as I was concerned.

"Oh. so you're a therapist now?" She chuckled.

I sat on the sofa and watched her as she put the milk, cheese, and orange juice in the refrigerator. "I guess I am," I said with a bit of cockiness, and then I smiled.

"Okay, smartass!" she replied as she grabbed a loaf of bread from a plastic bag and placed it in the bread container.

Before I could utter another word, the front door opened and Maggie's son Jamie walked into the house. "What's good, my boy?" I smiled, stood up, and gave him a fist bump.

"I'm good. Hungry though," he said.

"Is that my baby?" Maggie asked as she walked out of the kitchen to greet him. She stood in front of him with open arms as he approached her. I watched her as she hugged him. She was in her element. The way she treated her son was like a tiger protecting and loving her cub. For the most part, he could do no wrong in her eyes. And no one could talk bad about him while she was present because she would rip you a new asshole if you did.

I have only had a couple of man-to-man talks with Jamie. Thankfully, we squashed our run-ins because Maggie had a hard time dealing with 'em. The last thing I ever wanted to do was have her choose between me and her only kid. That would be a negative situation to be involved in. My job here was to make and keep her happy, and that's what I intended to do.

"Mom, are you cooking?" Jamie asked as she released her embrace.

"Do you want me to cook?" Maggie asked him as she headed back to the kitchen.

"Heck yeah," Jamie replied as he followed in her footsteps.

"Whatcha got a taste for?" she asked him as she stuffed the plastic bags used to carry her groceries into the top drawer near the dishwasher.

"Can you cook us some spaghetti?" Jamie asked as he grabbed a bottle of water from the refrigerator.

"I sure can," she happily agreed.

"Cool," he said while he screwed off the cap of the bottle of water. A couple seconds later he turned around and walked back in the living room where I was. "What's on TV?"

"Nothing really. The Lakers are playing later though," I told him.

"Yeah, I know. I may stick around and watch it. It depends on if Drake calls me. He's supposed to be getting some five-hundred-dollar Visa gift cards later, so I wanna get a couple of 'em."

"You just make sure that you bring one of those cards home to me," Maggie interjected from the kitchen.

"Come on, Ma, you know I got you," he assured her.

"You better," she said and cracked a smile at him.

"Where is he getting those cards from?" I inquired.

"From this girl he's messing around with. I think he said she's a manager at Target."

"How many is he getting?"

"I'm not sure. The last time he got some, she gave him ten of 'em."

"Did he break bread with Tommy Boy?"

"I don't know. He didn't say anything about it."

"You do know that if he didn't, and Tommy Boy finds out about it, he'll be reprimanded and sanctioned."

"Yeah, I know."

"Well, when you talk to him, remind him of it."

"A'ight," Jamie said, and then he took a sip of water from his bottle.

"You know the Rocket Boys just did a drive-by on the Iron Gang?"

"When?" I wanted to know.

"About thirty minutes before I got here. I don't know how true it is, but the dudes in the streets are saying that about six members got killed."

"You know the streets are gonna be hot tonight," I commented.

"Hell yeah, 'cause you know the Iron Gang ain't gonna sit down on that."

"Damn, nigga, you're acting like you're a fan of the Iron Gang," I replied sarcastically.

"Come on now, don't disrespect me like that. You know I don't fuck with those dudes. I'm just saying that the streets are about to get hot."

I cracked a smile. "Don't get in your feelings. I'm just fucking with you."

Jamie let out a sigh of relief. "Man, stop playing," he replied, and then he took another sip of water.

"Eddie, you better stop messing with my baby," Maggie said, coming to her son's rescue. She watched Jamie and me the entire time from the kitchen.

"I ain't messing with your baby. He's my son too, you know."

"Well, you better act like it," she commented, and then she turned her back to us and started preparing things so she could start cooking. Jamie and I continued to bond over gang affiliation talk and how we could create more hustles so we could get that paper. While we were chopping it up, Lily came knocking on the front door. Jamie let her in the house. She smiled and looked at him in a seductive way. "Hey, Jamie," she greeted him in a flirtatious way.

He smiled back at her. "What's up?" he replied as she brushed by him. He smacked her on her ass lightly.

"Boy, you better stop playing with me. You know I got that snapper," she commented as she passed him.

I watched her sway her hips from side to side as she walked across the living room floor. She glanced at me seductively, but Jamie didn't see it because her back was turned. I knew what she was doing. She liked the attention Jamie was giving her. She probably thought that she was making me jealous, but I couldn't care less. My only concern was that I didn't want Jamie to fuck with her. She wasn't the right type of woman for him. She was bad news; nothing more than a leech with a bunch of kids. She had different dudes running in and out of her crib every day. She was a liability and I needed to make him aware of that.

"Maggie, she's over here trying to borrow something else," I announced from the sofa.

"Oh, be quiet. I only need a stick of butter." Lily downplayed why she was here.

Maggie defended her from the kitchen. "Eddie, leave her alone. She's a single mother. I don't mind helping her from time to time."

Lily flicked her tongue at me and then she turned around and headed into the kitchen. Jamie sat back down on the couch and admired Lily from the living room sofa. "I'm gonna fuck her," he insisted, and took another sip from his bottle of water.

I tried to warn him. "Slow your roll, son. She's bad news."

"I've been trying to fuck her since she moved next door."

"Did you see all those kids she got?"

"I ain't trying to wife her up or be her kids' stepdaddy. I just wanna fuck her."

"She's gotta a lot of dudes running in and out of her crib. So you know she's got a lot of miles on her pussy."

"That ain't nothing that a condom can't cure."

"What if that condom breaks?"

"I can wear two of 'em." He sized her up while she was standing next to Maggie in the kitchen. "I mean, look at her ass. That shit is fat as hell," he pointed out.

"Yeah, and a bunch of other dudes said the same thing, that's why she got all those kids."

"Don't worry about me, I'm gonna be all right," he continued, salivating as he watched Lily. She knew he was watching her too, that's why she pranced around the kitchen. It seemed like the more I tried to talk him out of fucking with her, the more he persisted. All I could do was step back and let him do his thing. He was a grown man and I had to respect that.

8

TURNING TO THE STREETS—KHLOÉ

After watching that cop Brad Ford gallivant around with his mistress and then return home, I went to my next destination and that was the home of Chris Lemon. According to the information on this paper, he worked on the narcotics squad with Frances's husband for seven years. Judging from his photo, he looked like a nice guy. His facial features were similar to the actor Mark Wahlberg's. He also looked like he had served in the military. Army or marines, maybe. He lived in the city of Norfolk. Thirty miles away from his dirty colleague Brad Ford.

Chris Lemon also lived in a middle-class neighborhood. His home was at the end of a cul-de-sac, so there was no way that I could sit in my car to stake out his house without his neighbors seeing me. I did, however, get a look at the two cars in his driveway. There was a Honda minivan and a late model Dodge Charger. It did not take a rocket scientist to know that he was the owner of that Dodge Charger. The rims on the tires looked expensive. Two thousand dollar rims I might add. There was no way that he could have gotten them on a meager cop's salary. Didn't know if his wife knew what he was into. But it would be revealed once my investigation was over.

Knowing that I couldn't go any further here, I headed to the next man on my list, and that was Nicholas Witt. This white man also lived in Norfolk. He lived in Ocean View, which was a fifteen-minute drive from Chris Lemon's house. As I approached his residence, it was quickly revealed to me that he lived in an apartment complex. And it was a gated community. I needed a code to enter the premises. Once again, I found myself unable to continue my surveillance. I turned my car and headed to the house of the last cop on my list. His name was Ryan Lopez. He was a Latino. Frances didn't list how long he worked with her husband, but she put a message next to his name saying that he was the hothead of the group. He also looked like he was the youngest and the shortest of the squad, so in my mind, I was thinking that he felt like he had something to prove, that's why he went above and beyond the call of duty.

According to my GPS, he lived in Virginia Beach. But it wasn't that far from Chris's gated community. As a matter of fact, he lived near Shore Drive, which was only a twelve-mile drive. I headed in that direction. Halfway there, I noticed in my rearview mirror that a cop car was following me. It wasn't an undercover, it was a uniformed cop tailing me in his squad car. I closed my eyes to readjust them, but after I blinked my eyes to refocus them, I realized that I wasn't seeing things. I also saw that he had a partner in the car with him.

I let out a sigh. "Why are y'all following me? And what do you want?" I said aloud as I slid on my seat belt just in case they stopped me. Didn't want to give them the power to give me a ticket for not wearing my seat belt. After I secured my seat belt, the light flashed and the siren wailed from the police car and I was directed to pull my car over on the side of the road. I was parked on Little Creek Road in Norfolk and I could see the the Virginia Beach city line which was only a block away. The daring side of me told me that I should've kept driving but then I wondered what would've happened. The risk of getting arrested and being hauled off to jail seemed like a bad idea, so I waited for the cops to approach my car.

While I waited for them to engage me, I immediately noticed that I had all four cops' photos and information about them scattered around on the passenger seat of my car. I picked up my purse with my right hand and quickly dropped it on top of the pile of stuff sitting there.

"What are you doing there?" the cop on the passenger side of my car asked after he got within eye contact of my right hand. Instantly consumed with fear, I placed my hand on my right thigh and acted like I didn't know what he was talking about. "Put your hands on the steering wheel so that we can see them!" he instructed me. He yelled at me like we were in combat.

"What do you mean, what was I doing?" I asked. I swear, those were the only words that I could muster up to say.

The cop on my side of the car drew his police-issue pistol from his holster and pointed at my car. "You heard him! Put your hands where we can see them!" he roared.

"I'm doing it," I replied as I placed both of my hands on the steering wheel. "Why did y'all pull me over? I wasn't speeding," I added.

"Shut up! We'll ask the questions," the cop to my right said. "Now tell us what you were doing while we were walking to the car," he demanded as he peered into my car.

"I wasn't doing anything," I lied.

"You got any weapons in this car?" the cop to my left asked.

"No, I don't."

"Drugs?" His questions continued.

"No."

"Do you have your license and registration?" the cop to my right said.

"Yes, I do," I told him.

"Hand it to my partner." He instructed me.

I reached into my glove compartment, grabbed my registration, and then I grabbed my driver's license from my purse without moving it. "Here you go," I said and handed my credentials to the cop on my left.

"You're the news reporter," the cop to my left said after looking at my driver's license.

"I knew she looked familiar," the other cop commented.

"You live across town. What are you doing in these parts?" the same cop asked me.

"Taking care of business. That's all," I told him. "So, can I put my hands down now?"

"Why, sure you can," he said.

"Hey wait, is that a picture of Nicholas Witt?" the cop to my right inquired while looking farther into my car.

A sharp pain shot through my heart. I thought that I had covered everything up on the seat with my purse. I swear, I did not know what to do. I mean, I wanted to put my car in drive and haul ass out of there, but I knew I couldn't. Besides the fact that the cop to my left had my driver's license and car registration, I knew that they would catch up to me and then lock my ass up. So I did what everyone else would do in my situation and that was lie and pretend like I had no knowledge of who he was talking about. "I think you're mistaken. I don't know who Nicholas Witt is," I finally said.

"Don't play games with me, girl. That picture you got sticking up from underneath your purse is a narcotics detective named Nicholas Witt," the cop to my right insisted. He was not letting up.

"Since you know who I am, will you give me my license

and car registration back, so I can go?" I asked the cop to my left.

"Not until you move your purse and hand my partner that picture of Nicholas Witt."

"I know my rights. I don't have to show you anything," I protested.

"You know what, partner; I know she's lying because Detective Witt lives one mile south of here. She must've just left his residence," the cop to my right announced.

It seemed like my heart dropped into the pit of my stomach. I could not believe that I was in this situation. How the hell did I get here? I was just doing what I do, and then here came these freaking assholes. I needed to figure out a way to get out of this mess.

"Okay, listen, you guys. I was paid by a woman who's engaged to Nicholas to find out if he was cheating on her. That's it. So that's why I have a photo of him in my possession," I lied.

"I didn't know Nicholas was engaged. Did you, Frank?" the cop on the right asked the cop on my side.

"No, I didn't know that," they both said, clowning around.

"Well, he is. As a matter of fact, he just got engaged," I said, hoping I could get them to believe me.

"What's his fiancée's name?" the cop to my right asked.

"I'm not at liberty to say," I said. But I only said that because I could not think of a name that would sound plausible enough.

"I think we should call Nicholas ourselves and warn him that he's being watched," the cop to my left said, and chuckled.

"Yeah, I think we should too," the other one agreed.

"Okay, look, you two," I started off saying as I grabbed my wallet from my purse. I was so nervous, and it was noticeable because of the way I fumbled with my wallet trying to take the money from it. I finally was able to pull all the money from it. I had a total of two hundred dollars to my name, and I held it out to the cop on the driver side. "Here's all I have. You two can split it if you don't tell Nicholas that his fiancée hired me to follow him."

"Oh, so you're bribing us? Do you know that's against the law?" the cop to my left said.

"I think we should lock her up," the cop to my right said.

"Please, you guys. I mean no harm. Please do not arrest me. I am just trying to do my job. And besides, it's not like someone will find out. You guys haven't even gotten the statewide body cams for your uniforms yet."

The cop to my left looked around our immediate area and then he looked over the hood of my car. "Think we can use that money for lunch today?" the cop left of me asked.

"I don't think two hundred dollars is enough for us," the other cop replied.

"But that's all I have."

"I think we should take a trip to the nearest ATM," the other cop added.

"Yeah, that's a good idea," the cop standing at my window agreed.

"Okay, I'm fine with going to the ATM. There's one a block away in the parking lot of the Food Lion store."

"Yeah, there sure is. I'll tell you what, drive on over there and we'll catch up with you."

Relieved that these cops were going to let me off the hook if I went to an ATM and pulled out more money, it was like music to my ears. I watched both police officers in my rearview mirror as I drove back on the road. By watching their body language as they talked amongst themselves, I could tell that they were excited about how they had just come up on some free money. Whether they knew it or not, I was excited that I could bribe their crooked asses. I swear, there were so many fucking dirt-bag cops in this city. It wouldn't surprise me if the precincts in the neighboring cities were all crooked too.

The ATM was only a quarter of a mile from where the cops pulled me over. Getting there only took me three minutes, if that. I drove up to the drive-thru ATM and pulled out three hundred. With the two hundred that I had already had, that was a grand total of five hundred dollars. By the time I took the money from the ATM and retrieved my bank card, the cops were front and center. They still had my driver's license and registration, so the cop on the passenger side got out of the squad car, walked up to the passenger side of my car, and tapped on my slightly ajar window and tossed my credentials on the passenger seat. At that same time, I was instructed to place the money on the passenger seat.

"Have a nice day," he said.

"Hey, wait, you're not gonna tell Detective Witt, right?"

"My partner and I are going to think about it." He chuckled like what he was saying was funny.

"But I thought that we had a deal," I stated. I needed some clarity.

"I'll tell you what, don't let us see you in this part of town anymore. If we do, then all bets are off. I don't care who's paying you to investigate Detective Witt. Understood?"

"Yes, I understand," I replied. At this point, all I cared about was getting away from these crackers. I figured that if the other cop had seen all four pictures I had of their shyster-ass cop buddies, I would be up shit creek without a paddle.

When I got two miles into my drive, I became so frustrated at myself for messing this mission up. How did I drop my purse on top of my photos and stuff, but the cop was still able to see it? Ugh! What was I going to do now? I did know that I was in no mood to go to my next destination. I was too afraid that those cops might somehow follow me there. Damn! I screwed up! Ugh!

I beat myself up for messing things up all the way back to my apartment. After I went inside my place, it hit me that those cops never told me why they pulled me over. They never gave me an explanation. Whatever it was, I paid five hundred dollars for it. And now I was left with a bagful of questions and no one to answer them.

My uncle Ed called me, and that's when I realized that I had fallen asleep on my sofa with the television airing a marathon of *Keeping Up with the Kardashians*. I answered his call on the second ring. "Sounds like you were asleep," he pointed out.

"Yeah, I was. What time is it?" I asked, simultaneously looking at the clock on my cable box.

"It's a little after nine o'clock," he answered.

"I know, I see the clock now."

"So, are you coming out or what?"

"Yes, I'm getting up now."

"Had a long day?"

"You don't know the half of it. I was going to call you after I got in the house, but I dozed off, watching TV."

"Tell me about it when you pick me up."

"Okay. See you in thirty."

"See you in thirty," he said.

As soon as the call ended, my cell phone started ringing again. I looked at the caller ID and noticed that it was Frances calling me. I wasn't ready to talk to her right now, so I placed my cell phone flat down on my coffee table and got up. After five rings it stopped ringing. "Thank God she got the message," I commented as I walked towards my hallway bathroom. But as soon as I got within three feet of it, my cell phone started ringing again. I knew it had to be her calling, so I ignored it and did what I intended to do after I walked in the bathroom and sat down on the toilet. The entire two-and-a-half minutes that it took for me to pee, flush, and wash my hands, my cell phone rang over two dozen times. She called the first time and let the phone ring seven times. The second time the phone rang six times. The last two times, she let it ring another six times each. *I swear, if I don't nip it in the bud, this woman will end up running me crazy.*

It didn't take me long to grab my purse and head out. After I locked my front door, I raced to my car, simultaneously checking out my surroundings. I could never be too careful, especially after what happened to me earlier with those two cops. But nothing ever goes as planned.

Maybe tonight it would.

9

IN THE TRENCHES—UNCLE EDDIE

Maggie and I were sitting on the couch watching TV when I got a text from Khloé telling me that she was outside. So I grabbed my keys, told Maggie that Khloé was outside and that I was going to be gone for a couple of hours.

"Tell her I said hello," she instructed me.

"Will do, baby," I said and kissed her on her forehead.

"Be careful out there," she added.

"I will," I assured her, and then I made my exit.

On my way down the stairs that led to the parking lot, Lily was walking up the stairs. As soon as we were within arm's reach, she giggled. Before I commented, I looked up the stairs to see if Maggie was standing at the front door or the front window to our apartment.

"Whatcha looking back for? Wifey ain't watching us," she stated.

"I wasn't looking back to see if she was looking," I lied, trying to play it cool.

"Yeah, right, tell that shit to somebody else. You know I know what time it is. Just like I know that you were feeling some kind of way when her son Jamie was trying to holla at me earlier. I saw every facial expression you made. And you weren't feeling it."

"You couldn't have thought that. 'Cause I couldn't care less who you talk to. You don't belong to me," I said sarcastically and then I continued down the flight of stairs. I didn't even look back at that hoe. *She has clearly lost her damn marbles if she thinks that I care about who she's entertaining. I will be the first to say I do not.*

As soon as I got to the bottom step, I stepped down on the pavement and walked to Khloé's car. After I climbed in the passenger side and closed the door, I urged her to hurry up and get me out of this parking lot.

While driving away, she said, "Who was that?"

"A low-budget tramp with a houseful of bad-ass kids."

Khloé burst into laughter. "Sounds like you two have had relations."

"If that's what you wanna call it."

"You better be careful. You already know that you can't shit where you sleep. Women are treacherous. So, she could rat you out to Maggie at any time."

"I'd kill that bitch if she ever acted like she wanted to say something to Maggie."

"You better hope that she knows that," Khloé told me.

But I had had enough of talking about Lily's grimy ass and changed the subject. "So, you said you had some problems earlier."

"Yeah, but you won't believe what happened to me."

"Try me."

"Well, my day started off productive and it ended shitty," she started off. "Okay, so I was making my rounds. Doing my surveillance on all the cops. You know, watching their movements from my car, which was how I managed to follow that narco cop Ford when he went to meet up with his mistress. Now on to my second guy, Chris Lemon. When I got to his house, I realized that I could not stake out his place because he lived in a cul-de-sac, so I left. After I drove away, I headed to the cop Nicholas Witt's house, but that fell apart too because he lives in a gated community, so I left. Now this is where shit started falling apart. Two miles into my drive I look through the rearview and the freaking cops are following me. They pulled me over several seconds later. So, when they came to my car, they gave me the whole spiel about handing them my license and registration. Now while I'm going through my purse, the cop on my right looks in my car and sees one of the cops' pictures slightly sticking out from underneath my purse—"

I cut her off. "Where was your purse?"

"Where you're sitting now. So, when he saw it he asked me why did I have the cop's photo? I tried to deny it, saying that that wasn't who they thought it was. But they weren't going for it. They started threatening to call the cop and tell him that I had his picture. So I came up with this elaborate story about how I was hired by his fiancée to follow him to see if he's cheating on her."

"Did they buy it?"

"At first they didn't. And I was shaking in my boots too, because the only option I had left was to bribe them."

"No way."

"Yes, way, Uncle Eddie. I pulled out every dollar I had in my purse and handed it to the cop I gave my driver's license to."

"Did he take it?"

"I'm here talking to you now, aren't I?"

"How much was it?"

"Two hundred dollars."

"Wait, the cop took the money from you knowing that they have body cams?"

"You don't watch the news, do you?"

"Sometimes."

"The Virginia state budget didn't have enough money for body cams this quarter. All the police got to work with is the cams on their cars."

"Okay, so if the video cam was working on the cop's car, then how did they take the money from you?"

"He reached through my window and took it."

I chuckled because listening to my niece tell me how grimy these fucking cops were wasn't news to me. I knew how fucked up the cops were around here. Those motherfuckers were cowards with badges, and that's why dudes like me avoided them at all costs. "Did you get any guarantees for that money you gave them?" I asked her.

"I told them not to say anything. So I really don't know."

"Next time you have a run-in with the police, make them give you a guarantee. Got it?"

"Got it. So what's on the agenda tonight?" she wanted to know.

"I'm gonna take you to the streets and show you how to sit back and watch the police the right way," I said confidently.

She smiled at me. "All right, well let's do it." She pressed down on the accelerator harder and made her way down the boulevard.

The first spot I instructed her to go was the corner store off Tidewater Drive and Church Street. The narco cops hung out at that store and harassed every dope boy that came within yards of that spot. The cops even hung out at the projects around the corner called Young's Park. Let them tell it, it's their domain. But the dudes I ride with say something different.

When we pulled up to the corner store it was completely deserted. There was no one in sight but one of the neighborhood alcoholics standing in front of the store asking for change from every passerby.

"Pull up to that dude right there," I instructed Khloé, pointing at the old man.

Without saying a word, Khloé drove up to the guy so I could talk to him. When we came within a few feet of him I called him over to the car. I started off the conversation. "What's your name, dude?"

"Rick," he replied, and as soon as he opened his mouth, I got the biggest waft of alcohol. His body odor was much worse.

"What's up, Rick? Where's everybody at? Why you're the only one hanging out at the store?"

"The crackers came up here and cleared this shit out," Rick said.

"Which ones? Narcos or the blue boys?"

"The narcos."

"How long ago was it?"

"About fifteen minutes ago. I heard one of the corner boys say that they were out at Young's Park."

"A'ight, Rick, good looking-out, dude." I thanked him and then I reached in my pocket, grabbed a couple dollars and handed them to him.

"Thanks, young-blood," Rick said and then he walked off. Khloé and I watched him go in the store as she drove away.

"You know what he's going in there to do," she commented.

"A cold one," I replied.

"Exactly." She added, "So, are we going to Young's Park?"

"Yep, let's go. But make sure you stay back as far as you can from them crackers. They would love to snatch us out the car and rough us up for no damn reason."

"Okay," she said and drove in the ection of Young's Park. As soon as we pulled onto the main street of Young's Park, a couple of the Corner Boys were standing in a huddle, so I got Khloé to pull over to the curb. The Corner Boys were a small group of young dudes that's anywhere from twelve to nineteen years old that weren't strangers to carrying pistols, and they will pull them out without hesitation. So I hung my head out of the window to announce who I was as we approached them. It's also known around here in the streets that when it's dark and you don't announce who you are, you will get shot.

"Hey, y'all, this is Ed, have the narcs came through here?"

One guy spoke up. "Hell yah, they back there on the one-way, fucking with that nigga Rambo and his two brothers."

"They're probably round there robbing those dudes for their money and dope."

"That ain't nothing new. They're always taking dudes' shit. They took two grand from my homeboy and his girl last night after they pulled them over," one of the older boys said.

"Yeah, I had about twenty Percocets on me and four hundred dollars and they took it all from me," another kid said.

"Has the blue and white been out here?"

"Nah, we ain't seen them," the same guy said.

"A'ight, y'all dudes be careful."

"Don't worry, we're good," the older guy added.

"Let's go down the one-way," I instructed.

"Did you just hear that?" Khloé said as she drove away from the curb. "They just admitted that the cops take away their money and drugs and leave them on the streets. That's fucking insane, Uncle Ed."

"I told you that those crackers ain't shit. But you ain't seen nothing yet," I warned her.

Khloé drove towards the only one-way street in Young's Park, but halfway there a car sped towards us. The headlights were on high beam. They blinded me and Khloé for a moment, so she pulled her car over and put on the brakes. I pulled down the passenger-side sun visor to block the light while Khloé shielded her eyes with her arm. "That was them. That was Brad Ford and his boys." she pointed out.

"Wanna follow 'em?" I asked her.

"Of course I do, isn't that why we're out here?" she replied, and then she turned her car around to follow them.

10

NOT WHAT I EXPECTED—KHLOÉ

My adrenaline was pumping uncontrollably as I followed behind the narc cops' undercover car. Thankfully, they didn't go far because it would be hard to follow someone at night when there's only two to three cars on the street. Fortunately, they drove over to another housing authority. The low-income housing complex was called Kerry Park. It was directly across the street from Young's Park. The size of this place was almost the same size as Young's Park. It has always been known that when the cops clean the streets of the drug dealers from one housing project, the drug dealers flee to another one. So, I figured that this must be the case.

"Be careful, baby girl, you're driving too fast," my uncle advised me.

I took his direction and slowed my car down and pumped on my brakes a little. Driving as far back as I could, I gave the cops a distance of four hundred feet between us. But not that that mattered, because the cops had their sights set on a car parked curbside of the entryway of Kerry Park. I immediately pulled my car curbside a few feet back, and then I turned off my headlights.

"See that shit?" he asked me as he watched all four narco cops—Brad Ford, Nicholas Witt, Chris Lemon, and Ryan Lopez—wrangle one woman from a car.

"Why is he roughing her up like that? That's illegal."

"They don't care about that shit. I told you that those dudes are grimy."

"Do you see how he's patting her down?" I pointed out.

"If she was a guy, she would get treated worse than that," my uncle said. "Oh shit, they found something in her purse," he continued.

"But that's illegal search."

"Not for them."

"Somebody needs to call the police on them."

My uncle chuckled. "They are the cops."

"Oh, they found some money too."

"Oh, trust me, they're going to keep that. Everything they find they're going to keep it."

"I'm recording this," I said and pulled out my cell phone. It took me less than a second to activate the record button. I made sure that I zoomed in. "Looks like she's getting arrested. Isn't that Brad putting the handcuffs on her?"

"He ain't going to arrest her."

"But he's putting the handcuffs on her."

"They just want to get her out of the way."

I watched every move that Brad Ford made, and it was bothersome. The way he was treating that young woman was unfathomable. After he handcuffed her, he made her sit on the curb of the sidewalk.

"Do you see how they're all laughing at her? They are fucking pussies!"

"I think he just found the gun underneath the driver seat."

"Yep, that's a pistol," my uncle agreed after he witnessed

one of the cops holding a gun in the air. He was fanning it around like he was showing off a piece of jewelry.

"Look at that piece of shit fucking taunting her," I said angrily. I mean this guy was really getting on my nerves. As a matter of fact, all of them were getting on my nerves. They were making a mockery of her. And they were enjoying it. "I wonder how old she is?" I continued. My heart was going out to this young lady.

"She looks really young. Maybe twenty-one or twenty-two."

"How much time do you get for a gun?" I wanted to know.

"First offenders get anywhere between two to five years."

"Wait, what are they doing?" I asked as I watched Ryan Lopez and Brad Ford lift her up from the curb. Brad grabbed her by the arm and put her in the back of the undercover cop car.

"It looks like they're arresting her."

"Why did they take off her handcuffs?" I wondered aloud.

"That's a good question."

"I saw them put the gun and the money in the trunk of their car."

"That's nothing new. When they take something from you, they always put that shit in the trunk of their car."

"Ryan Lopez just got in her car and Nicholas Witt is riding with him," I announced, still holding my cell phone at an angle so I could record the whole thing.

"Look, Brad is making Chris drive their car while he gets in the back seat with that girl."

I cannot tell you why, but my heart was racing, watching these cops badger and arrest this young girl. I cannot tell you what they were about to do with her, but I was gonna stick around and find out. So as soon as both cars sped off in the opposite direction, I pulled off behind them to make sure that I drove quite a ways back so I would not be spotted.

"You know the routine, stay back as far as you can so those motherfuckers don't catch us following them."

As if I did not know that already, my uncle instructed me to fall back from tailing the cops before they got wind of us, so I fell back and decreased my speed without saying a word. I followed both cars as they traveled down the main driving strip of Kerry Park. When they reached the No Left Turn sign, they made a right turn and took the road that would either take you underneath the Berkley Bridge or to the ramp to the highway. I instantly was consumed with anxiety. "Think they're going underneath the bridge?" I asked my uncle.

"It looks that way," he replied.

"Whatcha think I should do?"

"You can't go underneath it with them."

"But the other road is going to take me across the bridge."

"Well, that's where we gotta go. Because I refuse to let you follow those crackers. You'll blow your cover."

"Why are they taking her to that dark-ass place? Think they're gonna kill her?"

"That's a good question. I just ain't got no answer for you."

"Well, we can't let them kill her."

"I'm not trying to get killed either. So, take the ramp," he demanded as he grabbed ahold of my steering wheel and jerked it to the left, just in time for me to go up on the ramp. But as soon as I got up on the ramp, I slowed my car down and pulled it over to the side of the road. "What the fuck are you doing?" he roared.

"I just can't let them take her underneath the bridge and not find out what they're gonna do to her," I protested after putting my gear in park.

"You can't back your car up."

I opened my car door. "Of course not, I'm gonna follow them on foot."

"No, I can't let you do that," he said and grabbed ahold of my arm. "I'll go," he insisted.

"So, whatcha want me to do?"

"Cross the bridge and take Berkley Avenue. Then make a U-turn and cross back over. But instead of taking Saint Paul's Boulevard, get off on Tidewater Drive and go to the spot we were at and I'll meet you there."

"Okay, but be careful."

"Don't worry about me. I've got all the protection I need," he assured me and showed me his gun that was tucked away in the waistband of his pants.

I put my car in drive and drove away after he closed the door. My heart was beating more uncontrollably than ever. My thoughts were tossing and turning throughout my brain too. I literally could not think straight. "Uncle Ed, please be careful," I said aloud although it was barely audible.

I was the type of person that always had to be in control. So, when I wasn't, I couldn't cope with my surroundings. I could only hope that things weren't what they seemed. And that I could go home tonight with a clear mind.

As instructed, I took the bridge and got off the Berkley Avenue exit, made a U-turn at the light, and drove right back across the bridge. I took the St. Paul's Boulevard exit and drove the speed limit back to the spot where we were when the cops snatched the girl out of her car. What I had to do now was wait.

11

TOO OLD FOR THIS SHIT—UNCLE EDDIE

I don't know how I ended up here. Sneaking and creeping around underneath a bridge just so I could spy on four loser-ass cops. I didn't tell this to Khloé, but I knew why those crackers were about taking homegirl back here. They were gonna rape her. I couldn't say how many of them were gonna do it, but I knew one of them was. That was Brad Ford's MO. He found a gun underneath her car seat and he found a nice piece of change in her purse, so her back was up against the wall. I knew that cracker gave her an option and she took the latter.

Underneath the Berkley Bridge was a nesting ground for homeless people. And even though a ton of them lived there, they didn't see shit. Dozens of people got killed underneath this bridge and ain't nobody ever seen shit. That's just how it was.

After walking for what seemed like half a block, I finally got within viewing distance of the cops' car, and the girl's car was parked directly in front of it. The tail of her car was facing the front of the cop's car. The area underneath the bridge was poorly lit. If it weren't for the moon lighting up the area, I wouldn't be able to see shit.

"We're gonna check the area out," I heard one of the cops say. That stopped me in my tracks. I hid behind one of the concrete slabs that held up the bridge. "Witt and Lopez, you go with them," I heard Brad Ford say.

"I'm already on it," that Lopez cop replied.

A few seconds later, I heard the crackling sounds of gravel. And all I could think about was that whoever was coming my way, was going to get his head cracked open. I would use my pistol to knock 'im out if I had to.

"I told you that the faster you do it, the faster you can get out of here," Brad said, "and I won't arrest you for having that gun."

"I told you that I can pay you." I heard her whimper like a lonely little dog. She sounded like she was about to break down.

"I don't want your money. I've got plenty of that. So be a good little girl and put it in your mouth slowly and then pull back on it. It's not hard to do. I'm sure you've sucked a life-time supply of black dicks, haven't you?" He pressed her, and all I could do was shake my fucking head. This cracker was so hard-pressed on getting that young girl to give him some head. To hear the way that he was talking to her sent my blood boiling. I swear, that if he didn't have those other three fuckers with him, I'd take off his fucking head.

I heard the girl whimpering louder. "Look, I've got herpes. And I just had a flare-up a couple days ago," she said.

"I think you're lying to me," I heard Brad say. "You know I could kill you down here and no one would even know it."

"Please don't kill me." She started begging for her life.

"Are you lying to me about having herpes?" he asked her.

She was quiet though. So he asked her again. "You better answer me, girl. Do you have herpes?"

She finally spoke. "No, I don't have it."

"Don't lie to me again. Do you understand me?" he scolded her.

"Sounds like she's giving you problems, boss man," I heard one of the other cops say, and then they all chuckled.

I didn't hear another word coming from that girl. But I heard Brad's voice. That motherfucker moaned and groaned the entire time that she sucked on his dick. I swear, it was unbearable to hear him raping her, while the other clowns laughed like the shit was funny. Damn, I wished that I could do something. But my hands were tied.

It took the girl around three minutes to get that asshole to bust a nut. And when he was done, he had the nerve to ask his flunkies if they wanted a turn. Every one of them declined to do so. Before they got in their unmarked cop car, I heard Brad Ford threaten to kill her and her family if she ever told anyone what happened. But it was too late, because I had heard it. And I wanted to make him painfully aware of it, but I knew I wasn't in a good position to take those fuckers out, so I decided against it.

Immediately after the cops got into their car and drove away, I called Khloé and told her that the cops had left and that it was okay to come and get me. While I waited for Khloé to come, I rode over to where the cops had left the girl. By this time, she was in her car, door closed, face buried in her steering wheel and crying her poor heart out. I knocked on her window lightly so I wouldn't scare her. But that mission failed, because as soon as she saw me, she started screaming at the top of her lungs and then she started up her car and put it in reverse. "Get away from me!" she screamed. "Get the fuck away from me!" she continued, and then she put her foot on the accelerator and sped out of there like a bat out of hell. And she did this while her car was in reverse. I thought she was going to back into one of the concrete slabs, but she didn't. She was out of there within two to three seconds. This shit happened so fast.

I stood there alone in the dark waiting for Khloé to show up. But then I remembered that there were people near where I was standing. I heard someone clear their throat and it sounded like it was a man. Then I heard two people whispering. I couldn't gauge whether it was two men or a man and woman talking because of the noise coming from the cars crossing the bridge. "Hey, did y'all see what happened?" I asked whoever was listening.

"Did you see what happened?" one homeless person said. I could instantly tell that the voice came from the person who cleared their throat.

"Yeah," I replied.

I wanted to see if this guy would say something else, but he went radio silent on me. "Did the other cops know that y'all were out here?"

"Where are we gon' go? This is our home," the same homeless guy replied.

"Yeah, a'ight," I said, and then I started walking towards the street. And as soon as I started walking, Khloé's headlights were approaching me. I met her at the curb as she pulled over. She wouldn't let me get in the car and close the door before she started grilling me.

"So, what happened? Did they take her to jail?" she asked as she sped off from the curb.

"Nah, Brad took her underneath that bridge and made her suck his dick."

"No fucking way! Please tell me that you're kidding me."

"I wish I was."

"So, all of the cops made her do that?" Khloé asked me. She was very alarmed by the thought of it.

"Nah, just that cracker Brad. Yo, I swear to God that if he

was alone making her do that shit to him, I would've killed that nigga with my bare hands."

"What was she doing? Was she doing it willingly? What?"

"No, she begged him not to do it. She told him that she'd pay him. But he said he didn't need her money. And threatened her that if she didn't do it, she was going to jail."

"So, did you see her actually sucking him off?"

"No, it was too dark. But I heard that rapist-ass cracker moaning and shit like they were in a fucking hotel or some shit. Yo, I've seen and heard some grimy shit in my life, but that shit I just heard fucked me up."

"Where is she now? Did she leave?"

"After they left her, I walked over to her car so I could talk to her, but when I knocked on the window, she started screaming, talking about leave her alone and then she hauled ass out of there. So, after she drove off, I heard a couple of bums talking and shit. I even heard one of them clear his throat, so I asked him did he see what happened? And he threw the question back at me and I said yeah. Then I asked him if the cops knew that he and the other ones knew that they were out there, and he said, where are we going to go?"

"No way. He said that?"

"Yep. See, the cops do what they want to do because they know the homeless people ain't testifying against them. All they care about is where they're gonna lay their heads and where they're gonna get their next meal. If it's a wino, you can forget it, they'll never come to court. The cops will either make 'em disappear or they'll disappear on their own."

Khloé looked like she had a lot more questions, but her cell phone rang and distracted her for a brief moment. "Fucking worrisome-ass bitch!" she mumbled, and then she placed her phone in the cup holder. "I cannot believe that he made her suck him off. He's a sick-ass monster!"

"Well, believe it, because it happened."

"Wonder if she's gonna tell anyone."

"I doubt it. I heard him threaten to kill her and her family if she opened her mouth."

"*Arrrgggggg* . . . you heard him say that?" Khloé sounded shocked.

"Yeah, I heard him say that."

"I gotta get his ass off the streets. All three of his minions too. They're probably sucking his dick too!"

After the incident with the narcs and hearing about what happened to the young girl, Khloé decided that she wanted to go home. I was all for it. I wanted this day to be over. Get some much-needed rest because of all the running around I did earlier today. Immediately after I told Khloé to take it easy and drive home safe, I got out of the car and watched her as she drove out of the parking lot.

On my way up the two flights of steps that I needed to climb to get to my apartment, I had to pass by Lily and Jamie. "Back so soon?" Jamie commented as he stood up with his back against the metal rail. Lily was standing in front of Jamie, playing touching and feeling games with him. She even leaned in and kissed him on his neck.

"Yeah, my niece needed me to make a run with her. And it ended sooner than we thought it would," I answered while watching Lily playing mind games.

"You know I told you that if you kiss me again, I'm taking you into my crib," Jamie warned her.

"I told you only a grown man can handle this," she teased.

I shook my head and turned my attention towards getting to my front door. Thankfully I was only a few feet away from it. "Jamie, be careful out here. You know niggas from other sets love to catch a nigga off guard," I reminded him.

"I'm good, Ed. You know another dude will never catch

me slipping. I got eyes in the back of my head," he said casually, keeping his eyes on Lily.

"If you say so," I replied, and then I went into the apartment.

Maggie was nowhere in sight. I heard the shower water running, so I realized that she was taking a shower. I grabbed a cold bottle of Corona from the refrigerator and took a seat on the sofa. The eleven o'clock news was on, so I lay back and watched it.

12

THE DEVIL IS A LIAR—KHLOÉ

I couldn't shake the thought of those freaking cops making that poor girl perform oral sex on 'em. I could only imagine how degraded she felt. Fucking bastards! *I will make them pay for sure.*

When I pulled up and parked my car outside my apartment, I turned off the ignition and sat there quietly. I wondered what kind of sick world I was living in. I knew that there are good and evil people. I knew that there are positive and negative effects in every situation. My only issue was that, when does it all stop? We've gotta stop hurting each other because it's just not right.

While in deep thought about my plans tomorrow, I saw a dark shadow appear in my side-door mirror. I blinked my eyes to refocus them. And when I opened them, I came face-to-face with Frances. Cradling my breasts with both of my hands, I stared her down. "Why the fuck did you scare me like that?" I yelled.

"Look, you left me no choice. I've been trying to call you and you've been ignoring my calls," she explained sarcastically.

I opened my car door and got out of the car. "I was going to call you when I got home," I lied. She wasn't going to hear from me until the following day.

She cut to the chase. "Have you been working?"

I closed my car and clicked the alarm button from my car key. "All of this micromanaging isn't gonna speed things up," I replied.

"You call it micromanaging, I call it minor updates," she said as she followed me towards my apartment.

I sighed.

"So, any news?" She would not let up.

I sighed once more. This time it was heavily. "Can you wait until I get inside my apartment?"

"Yes, sure," she agreed as she walked alongside of me. It took us less than twenty-five seconds to unlock my front door and enter my apartment. And as soon as I turned on the light in the living room, I stood there and watched Frances as she surveyed the immediate surroundings. "This is cute. Small but cute," she said, complimenting the décor she could see.

"Thirsty?" I asked her after I tossed my handbag and car keys on the table I use to place my mail on.

"No, thank you."

"Have a seat," I suggested after grabbing the remote from the coffee table and powering on the television.

"Thank you," she replied. "You live here alone?"

"I do now," I said. In reality, I knew she was trying to fish information from me about my private life.

"How long?" She would not let up.

I headed to the bathroom, pretending not to hear her question. I had been holding my bladder for a couple of hours now, so I had to release it and do it quickly. After I washed my hands, I reappeared.

"How long have you been single?" she did not hesitate to ask me after I exited the bathroom.

"For a little over a year," I told her. I cannot tell you how I came up with that number. I guess it just popped into my head.

"Did he cheat on you?" Her questions kept coming.

"No. We just decided to part ways," I lied once again as I stood in the middle of the living room floor.

"Well, just be grateful that he wasn't murdered," she commented.

"You know it's not a good idea to be staking out my neighborhood. My neighbors are nosey and leery about strange people roaming around in this neighborhood. They'll call the cops on you without hesitation," I told her.

"I guess God is on my side, huh?" she said. But then her facial expression changed. It looked somewhat wicked. A grimace almost. "You said you were going to tell me something after we came into your house," she reminded me.

I took a seat on the sofa across from her. I hesitated, trying to gather my thoughts. Battling with the decision if I should tell her about what I witnessed tonight. I wanted to make sure that I gave her the proper amount of information but without casting doubt in her mind that I could handle this job that she paid me to do.

She pressed me. "Are you okay?"

"Yes, I'm fine."

"Well, give me an update."

I took a deep breath and then I said, "Those cops you hired me to investigate are savages. I've seen a lot of things during my journalism career at the network, but this takes the cake."

"What happened?"

"I witnessed the whole gang of them harass a young girl. They pulled her over and found a gun in her car. And at that point they gave her the option to go to jail or perform oral sex on 'em. Unfortunately, she choice the latter and found herself sucking off Brad underneath the Berkley Bridge."

"Hold up, you saw that?" She wanted clarity.

"Yes, I did," I lied. I could not divulge the fact that my uncle was there.

"Did you get any pictures . . . photos of it?"

"It was too dark. I heard the dialog between the young girl and the cops."

"See, didn't I tell you that those guys were monsters?" she pointed out as she rotated her head back and forth.

"Sitting here visualizing the images in my head is becoming unbearable," I mentioned.

"If they did that to that girl, just imagine how many others."

"I asked myself the same question."

"So, what's the plan now? You know time is winding down."

"Yes, I'm aware of that."

"Do you have one of those professional cameras? Private investigators use them all the time. The functionality of it would be awesome and it would help you spy on those assholes really easy. Just think how quickly you'd be able to get more dirt on them."

"No, I don't have one of those, but the equipment I do have will work just fine," I assured her.

"Look, if you don't have one because of the price, I could go and get one for you," she offered.

"No, I'm fine. I've got everything I need."

"Those cameras have the night-vision capabilities. If you would have had one with you tonight, you would've been able to record those rapists in action," she pointed out.

As much as I wanted to tell her that I was not there but my uncle was, that would show my level of incompetence and it would further let her know that I had someone with me. So I just sat there and let her harp about this fucking camera. She pointed out how it could cut my time of investigating in half. She also reminded me once again about my deadline. So, after sitting there and listening to her endless tirade about the stupid camera, I agreed to let her purchase me one. "Okay, let's do it."

"Do what?" she replied.

"Get the camera," I told her.

"Really?" Her tone changed. Her face lit up like a Christmas tree.

"Yes, get me the camera."

"Okay. Awesome. I'm gonna be at the top P.I. store as soon as they open tomorrow morning. So please be available when I call you to meet up with me."

"What time will that be?" I reluctantly asked her.

"Let's say, ten o'clock."

"Sounds great," I said as I watched her stand up.

"Please answer my call when I call you in the morning," she instructed me with a questionable facial expression. From the way I dodged her calls today, I knew where her skepticism came from.

"Don't worry, I will," I tried to assure her after I stood up from the sofa and casually walked towards her. "Be careful out there," I warned her.

"I will, thank you," she replied, and then she exited my apartment.

I watched her as she walked to her car. While my eyes were fixed on her safety and well-being, I could not help but think about the kind of husband she'd had. Was he a good guy or what? And his role in this cop clique of his. I even thought, was he capable of taking his own life? I guessed time would reveal those answers.

The moment after Frances got in her car and drove away, I moseyed down the hallway and into my bedroom. I collapsed on my bed with intentions to get a one-hour nap and then get back up, take a hot shower, and then close my eyes for the rest of the night. That did not happen though. My cell phone alarm woke me up at eight o'clock. The sun from outside my window added more pressure to get me out of the bed.

"Come on, Khloé, we got things to do today," I coached myself, and then I turned over on my bed and proceeded to get up. I could not even get out of my bed before my cell phone rang. The ring was not that loud, so I knew that I had not brought it to my bed with me last night. When the third ring chimed, I remembered that I had left it in my purse from the night before. I rushed to my living room and grabbed my cell phone from my purse on the table near my front door. I instantly looked at the caller ID and saw that it was Frances. "Why the fuck are you calling me right now? You said that you were going to call me around ten o'clock," I said to myself, clenching my teeth while contemplating whether or not to take the call.

The fifth ring forced me to do so. "Hello," I finally said, and then I flopped down on my living room sofa. "I was using the bathroom," I lied. Lying to her had become an easy thing to do.

"I was beginning to think that I was gonna have to make another trip to your apartment."

"Listen, Frances, making the trips to my apartment isn't necessary. You paid me to help you investigate your husband's death and his former comrades, so please let me do my job," I pleaded with her. I was honestly becoming more annoyed by the minute with this lady. There was no winning with her.

"Tell you what, do your job, check in with me on a daily basis, and I won't have to make a home visit," she replied sarcastically.

Instead of cussing this woman out, I took a deep breath and exhaled. "You got a deal," I uttered through clenched teeth.

"Great," she said.

"Is there another reason why you called me this early? Remember you agreed to call me around ten o'clock after you left the P.I. shop," I reminded her.

"Oh yeah, you're right. I was calling to ask you if you'd meet me down at the store, that way if you have any questions on how to use the camera, one of the store clerks can give you one-on-one instructions."

"Sorry. I won't be able to meet you. Gotta make a pharmacy run for my grandmother. And then I've got to help her write a few checks to pay her bills." I lied once again. I was trying to come up with every excuse I could muster. As far as I was concerned, the less time I spent with her, the better off I would be. "Just gather what information you can, and whatever I can't figure out, I'll get my old camera guy from the station to show me how to operate it."

"Oh no, that's not a good idea. He's gonna wanna know why you need help in trying to operate the camera, and then it's all gonna lead back to me." Frances became uptight.

"Frances, you gotta calm down. Everything is going to be okay. Let me handle my end of this job and you do the same on yours," I told her.

"Okay, but no hiccups. Got me?"

"Yes, I got you."

"All right, be available at ten o'clock when I call you."

"I will."

"Awesome. See you then," she said, and we ended our call.

After what happened last night with the girl and the cops, I knew that I had to come up with a different way to gather my intel. Now, I knew that I'd covered and investigated far worse things, like murders and kidnappings, but that young girl didn't deserve to be treated that way. I knew now that getting those cops off the streets was necessary. No matter what I had to do.

Once I took a long, hot shower, I slid into a T-shirt and a pair of sweatpants. While I was boiling hot water to make myself a cup of tea, my cell phone started ringing again. I looked at the caller ID and realized that the call was coming from my uncle Eddie. "Hey, Unc, what's going on?" I greeted him after I took the call.

"I'm more concerned about you, especially after what happened last night. I wanted to call you, but I figured that if you wanted to talk, then you'd call me."

"Yeah, that situation has been toying with my heart-strings. It's like, I'm angry at one point and then my emotions switch and then I start feeling sorry for the poor girl."

"That's just how life rolls. It's a dog-eat-dog world. I've been on this earth for a long time, and nothing fazes me. If you had been to the places I've been, then you'd know why my skin is so tough."

"Being a journalist and investigating stories from the streets that I was raised up in kinda prepared me for the stuff like what happened last night. But then again, when I find out that a woman or children are involved, my emotions get the best of me and then I'm a pool of water."

"Look, baby girl, just look at it this way: The quicker you get those motherfuckers off the street, the less you'll have time to cry."

I chuckled at my uncle because he was right. My mission was to do the job I was paid to do and leave the scraps on the streets.

"So, what's on the agenda today?" he wanted to know.

"I'm meeting the cop's wife in about thirty minutes to pick up a professional-grade camera and video device. I told her about what happened last night. And while she's happy that I saw firsthand how those cops operate, she was bummed out that I didn't get that footage on camera. So, to prevent that from happening again, she's at a P.I. store picking up what I'm sure is a very expensive camera, and as soon as she leaves the place, we're gonna meet up."

"I don't think that was a good idea telling her about the shit that happened last night."

"Believe me when I tell you that I didn't want to. She showed up at my apartment last night and damn near forced it out of me."

"Wait, hold up. She showed up to your place last night?"

"Yeah, she did. Remember I kept getting call after call last night?"

"Yeah."

"That was her. She wants me to give her an update on everything I find out on a daily basis. And since I refused to answer her calls yesterday, she took it upon herself to show up at my apartment."

"Khloé, that's not good. What if those crooked-ass mother-fuckers are watching her and decide to follow her and then they see her with you? Everybody in the Tidewater area knows who you are. You just helped solved that murder case for the homicide cops not even five days ago. She needs to chill the fuck out and get a grip on herself."

"I've already expressed that to her. But she won't listen."

"Do you want me to tell her? Because you know I would."

"I'll tell you when I see her this morning."

"Let her know that if she doesn't stop stalking you, then I'm gonna intervene."

"She doesn't know that I've got you working along-side me."

"Well, she will know if she doesn't cut that bullshit out! I'm not playing, Khloé, let that bitch know that she can't be toying with your life."

"I will. I will." I tried reassuring my uncle. Eddie could be a loose cannon at the drop of a hat. Trips back and forth to prison only made him worse. With that in mind, I was gonna need to pick and choose my words when I discussed the matters of this case. That is, until I closed it.

Uncle Eddie and I talked for a few more minutes. In those

couple of minutes, I gave him the heads-up that I'd come by his place before the sun set. Once he agreed, we ended the call. But as soon as I set my cell phone down on the coffee table in the living room, it started chiming. Without looking at the caller ID, I knew the call was coming from Frances. "Hello," I said.

"I picked up the goodies and I'm outside your apartment building."

I turned around, looked back at my front door, stood up from the sofa, and rushed toward the window next to my front door. "Where are you? I can't see you," I announced as I surveyed the front yard of my apartment.

"I'm getting out my car right now. I'm wearing a green polo shirt. See, I'm waving at you," she stated. When she told me what she was wearing, I immediately zoomed in on her.

"Yes, I see you," I replied in a nonchalant manner. And before she could utter another word, I ended the call.

Was this bitch crazy or what? We had agreed that we'd meet on the streets, not at my freaking apartment. *I see right now, I'm gonna have to give her a piece of my mind.*

As soon as I heard her footsteps outside my front door, I opened it. She was smiling from ear to ear, holding up a white plastic bag with a medium-size box inside. "I picked the most expensive digital camera they had in the store," she bragged.

I smiled back at her. But on the inside, I was turned off by her antics. The more and more I was around her, the more aggressive she became. "Aren't you gonna let me in?" She questioned me in a sarcastic manner.

"Sure, come on in," I replied.

I stepped to the side so she could cross the threshold to enter my apartment. After she passed by me, I looked outside to make sure no one had followed her, and when I saw that the coast was clear, I closed the front door and locked it.

"You will not believe the money I spent," she declared

boastfully as she sat down on my sofa. She placed the bag on the coffee table in front of her and then she pulled the box out of it. "This is a top-of-the-line camera." She added, "It's a Canon EOS R5. The guy that sold this to me told me that it's a high-resolution, high-speed camera with video capabilities. It has a full-frame mirrorless feature and the dual pixel autofocus installed in here is the latest generation."

"I can't believe that you remembered all that," I commented, and then I took a seat next to her.

"Here, take a look at it." She handed the camera to me. "You don't have to do anything. The store clerk already powered it on. He initiated the settings and all you have to do is either take a picture or use it to record."

I turned the camera over and over to get a better look at it. I played with the functions of it as well. "How much did you say this cost?" I asked her.

"Just a little over three thousand dollars. And the clerk, he said that we're gonna get our money's worth from it," she boasted.

"Why did you spend so much?"

"When it comes to matters of my husband, money is not an issue. And besides, you only have just a few days left on your deadline."

Frances struck a nerve inside me, so I placed the camera on the coffee table and turned my full attention towards her. "Look, Frances, you don't have to keep reminding me about the deadline you gave me. I know what I am supposed do and the time I have to do it, so stop putting pressure on me. I know what I am doing."

"If you knew what you were doing, you would've gotten those clowns on tape last night and I wouldn't have had to go out and buy this three-thousand-dollar camera."

"I didn't ask you to go out and get this camera. You did this on your own," I reminded her. "As a matter of fact, you do a lot of shit on your own, because I told you that I'll meet you somewhere on the streets. But no, you decided that you were going to do what Frances wants to do and brought your ass over here."

"So, my coming here is a problem for you?"

"Of course it is. I don't pop up at your house."

"You could."

"That's not the point. We cannot be seen together. What if those cops decide to follow you and then see you with me? There's no telling what could come of that, especially since I just helped the homicide detectives solve that murder."

"You need to stop being paranoid. Those misfits you are talking about threatened to file a restraining order on me because I used to show up on their doorsteps almost every day, demanding them to give me answers about my husband's death. So, them following me around town is a far stretch."

"Even if they did threaten to file a restraining order on you wouldn't stop them from hiring a private investigator like you did."

Frances sucked her teeth. "You're reading too much into this. But I'll tell you what, I won't come to your place anymore, just as long as you answer all my calls and give me a daily briefing. Deal?"

Reluctantly, I agreed.

"Okay, awesome," she replied, and then she stood up from the sofa. "This meeting here doesn't count as a daily briefing, right?"

"No, this doesn't count as a briefing," I assured her.

"What time can I expect to talk to you?"

"Eleven o'clock tonight. No later than midnight."

"Perfect," she said, and then she walked to my front door. I stood up from the sofa and followed her.

"Remember, we only have three days left," she reminded me after she opened my front door.

"Yes, I am aware of that," I concurred.

"Talk to you later," she responded, and then she exited my apartment.

Normally I would watch my visitors leave my place and close my door after they drove away, but this chick wasn't a visitor. She was an intruder. An intruder that would be out of my hair three days from now, and I could not wait.

13

OUTCAST—UNCLE EDDIE

I hopped in the shower after I got off the phone with Khloé and immediately after I got dressed, I grabbed the plate of food Maggie had waiting for me in the microwave. She was already sitting down at the kitchen table eating when I entered the kitchen, so after I grabbed my plate from the microwave, I took a seat at the table across from her. "This looks really good," I commented after looking down at a plate of turkey bacon, cheese eggs, and cubed fried potatoes.

"I also know what to say," she replied and chuckled.

"Happy wife, happy life," I recited like I read it from a book.

Maggie's smile grew bigger. "So, whatcha getting into today?"

"Nothing right now. But I am gonna get up with Khloé later though."

"Tell me what you and her got going on?" She questioned me while chewing a forkful of the potatoes from her plate.

I was chewing a mouthful of cheese eggs when I answered her. "Nothing to call home about," I said, trying to downplay the mission that my niece and I were working on.

"Now, I know that you love your family, but at the same time, I want you to keep in mind that your family could be your downfall. And Khloé is at the top of that list."

"It's no different from being in a gang all my life."

"It's a lot different. And the guys that are around you every day are talking about it."

Shocked by Maggie's statement, I placed my fork on my plate and looked at her. "What guys?" I didn't hesitate to ask. The blood traveling through my veins started boiling. In my head, I was thinking, *Why the hell are dudes I call my brothers talking about me?* And then to be talking about me to my girlfriend was a major violation.

"Who is it?" I asked her. "And why the fuck are you letting them talk about me behind my back?" I roared. I was on edge.

"First of all, I'm gonna need you to bring your tone down. You know I wouldn't let anyone disrespect you, especially in my face."

"Well then, what happened? Who was running their mouths about me?" I pressed the issue.

"Jamie heard a couple of the young guys talking about you after you left the spot the other day."

"Who was it?"

"Some new guy that just got initiated."

"What's his name?"

"I don't know. Ask Jamie."

I was furious. The disrespect from a little dude that just got inducted into our gang, talking about an OG in that fashion, ain't cool. Didn't he know that I would break his neck? I would do it in a heartbeat and come home and get a night's rest.

"Where is Jamie now?"

"He's in his room."

I stood up from the kitchen table. "Jamie!" I yelled from the kitchen. But he didn't answer, so I called him again. "Jamie!"

"He's probably asleep. He was hanging out with Lily all last night," Maggie added.

"Well, he's about to get up right now," I announced, and stormed out of the kitchen. By the time I got to Jamie's bedroom, the door opened and he peered around the door.

"What's wrong?" he asked. His voice was groggy. He wiped both eyes with the back of his hands.

"Your mama just told me that some little dude from our camp was talking shit about me."

"Yeah, he did, but it wasn't nothing really."

"What the fuck you mean that it wasn't nothing? He violated one of our codes. It's forbidden to talk shit about an OG in our organization."

"Come on, Ed, the lil dude was just joking around."

"You let me be the judge of that," I said, gritting my teeth together. "What else did he say?"

"He was just saying that he couldn't believe that your niece was a rat, and if you ever put a bounty on her, he's gonna volunteer because he's gonna hit it before he lay her down."

"That little dude said that bullshit and you thought that he was joking around?"

Maggie walked up behind me. "Why are you screaming at him? He's just the messenger."

"I'm not screaming at him. I'm just trying to get an understanding why he thought that little nigga was joking when he said that my niece was a rat. But that ain't it, he said that if I ever put a bounty on her head, he'll do it but that he's gonna fuck her first."

"A'ight, you're right. What he did was wrong, so I told him to chill."

"Did you tell him that she was off limits?"

"Yeah, I did. I told him that she's family and she ain't no rat."

"And what did he say?"

"He was like, a'ight . . . a'ight."

"Why didn't you come and tell me?"

"Because I knew that you would act like this."

"What's this dude's name?"

"Bryan. His nickname is Bullet."

"What does he look like?"

"He's a dark dude, just a little bit taller than me. And he got a head shaped like a bullet."

"Was anyone else around when he made those comments?"

"Yeah."

"Who?"

"Miles was there. Apple Head was there. Oh, and Lee was there too."

"What did they say?"

"They was telling him to chill too."

"Yeah, a'ight. Get dressed."

"Where we going?" Jamie wanted to know.

"We're going to the spot."

Jamie sucked his teeth and let out a long sigh. "I knew I shouldn't have opened my big mouth," he said, and then he slammed his bedroom door shut.

"Please don't go out of here and do something," Maggie warned me as I turned around and walked by her.

"I won't," I told her. Pumping with a high adrenaline rush, I slipped on a pair of sneakers, grabbed my pistol from underneath the mattress in my bedroom, and then I grabbed my car keys and stormed out of the house. I waited four minutes, and Jamie finally came outside and got in the car.

"You know I'm gonna be considered a rat after you confront Bullet," Jamie mentioned while I was exiting the parking lot.

"Fuck that nigga! Anytime a dude talk about family, then he's considered an outcast!" I shouted at him. I needed him to get it through his head that that type of behavior isn't tolerated. I don't care if a dude is playing or not, some things just aren't accepted.

Jamie and I rode in silence the whole ride to the spot in Park Place. And as soon as I parked my car curbside, Jamie got out first. He walked ahead of me and I followed. After I walked into the spot, I was greeted by Tommy Boy and Jay. They were on their way out the front door. We shook hands and gave the back pat as we always did when we greeted each other.

"Everything good?" Tommy Boy asked me while Jay stood behind him. We were all standing there in a huddle.

"I'm looking for that Bullet."

"He just left. Him and Apple Head went up the block to the corner store," Tommy Boy informed me.

"What is he wearing?"

"A blue Notre Dame hoodie."

"A'ight," I said, and then I turned around to walk back out the spot.

"Is everything a'ight?" he asked me.

"He said some disrespectful shit about Khloé, so I'm gonna check him on it."

"A'ight, well, take care of your business and holla at me later," Tommy Boy insisted.

"Will do," I assured him, and then I walked out the front door and left.

I had the intentions to yell and tell Jamie to come with me, but I was too angry and focused on coming face-to-face with this fucking idiot, so I kept it moving.

My heart started racing uncontrollably as I sped away from the spot. I saw Tommy Boy talking to Jay as they walked to his car. I can't say what they were talking about, but when I saw Tommy Boy shaking his head, I knew he knew that I was on a mission and I wasn't gonna hold back when I walked up on this Bullet cat.

The corner store where I was told that Bullet was, was only two blocks away, so I drove down the first block slowly. Inside my head I was thinking about how I was going to handle this little nigga when I saw him. One part of me wanted to pistol-whip his ass. But the other part of me wanted to scare the living hell out of him and make him promise me that he will never do that shit again.

While trying to figure out how I was going to run up on this dude, he showed up on my radar. He and that dude Apple Head were on the left side of the street, walking in my direction. We were in Park Place, and this section of Norfolk had a lot of one-way streets and I was driving down one of them. I pulled my car over when I got within three hundred feet of them. "A yo, Bullet, let me holla at you," I shouted.

He looked in my direction, and he looked nervous when he saw that it was me calling him. He slowed down his pace and so did Apple Head as they walked towards my car. I was going to instruct Apple Head to go back to the spot alone, but I wanted him to learn from this lesson that I was going to throw Bullet's way.

While they were walking towards me, I looked Bullet in the eyes before he put his head down. He looked worried.

Fear was written all over his face. He looked like a weak-ass little boy. I figured if he looked that way to me, then he'd look like a pussy in other gang members' eyes. And he would put my soldiers in danger. Tommy Boy and I were gonna have another sit-down when he got back to the spot.

"Hey, OG," Apple Head greeted me after he and Bullet got within three feet.

"What's up, OG?" Bullet said as he stood alongside of Apple Head.

"Nigga, don't *what's up, OG* me!" I gritted my teeth at him and then I got out of my car. I wanted to stand toe to toe with this clown. "I heard you had a lot to say about my niece the other day. So now I need you to repeat everything you said to those niggas, to me," I continued as I stood before him.

"I don't remember everything I said," he started off saying.

"Man, I ain't trying to hear that shit. You told a roomful of niggas that my niece was a rat and you'd murk and rape her if I gave you the order," I snarled.

"Nah, OG. I didn't say that." He lied.

"Apple, did you hear this nigga disrespect my niece, Khloé?"

Apple Head hesitated, looking at Bullet and then looking back at me. That alone gave me the confirmation that Bullet did just what Jamie said.

"Nigga, why you taking so long to answer my question? Tell me, did you hear him talk shit about my niece!" I snapped.

"Sorry, OG, but I ain't no rat! You gotta ask him," Apple Head insisted. "As a matter of fact, this ain't none of my business." He turned and began walking away.

"Nigga, where the hell you think you going? You don't walk away from me when I'm talking to you!" I roared. I could not believe that this little dude had the heart to disrespect me and then walk off like I wasn't talking to him.

"Yo, Apple, do you hear me?" I stood there, furious, trying to hold my composure because this dude was embarrassing the crap out of me and he was doing it in front of a new member of our organization. I mean, Bullet had only been in our gang for a couple weeks, so Apple Head was really making me look real lame. Like I had no rank, or no authority, and I could not have that. What example was I showing right now? It was not good.

Without giving it a second thought, I shot off behind him, grabbed my pistol from the waist of my pants, aimed it Apple Head, and then I pulled the trigger. *Boom! Boom! Boom!* It happened so fast, but it happened in slow motion. I saw the flame spark from the barrel of the gun and then Apple Head collapsed to the ground. I stood there and watched the blood drain from his head into a pool around it.

By the time I looked back at Bullet, he had run off in the opposite direction. I saw the back of his hoodie vanishing around the side of a house halfway down the block. I could not believe that this dude could run so fast. He was my main target, so I left Apple Head to die while I hopped back into my car and sped off in the direction that he ran. As I approached the house he disappeared around, I slowed down so I could get a quick look. But he was not there.

Because of what just happened, I knew I had to call Tommy Boy, since he was the leader of this gang. I just hoped that he understood why I handled this situation the way I did. More importantly, I could not let him find out what I did from someone else. That would be blatant disrespect on all levels. So immediately after I made a right turn at the corner, I grabbed my cell phone from the cup holder and dialed his number. He answered on the second ring. "Yo, G, what's up?" he asked me.

"Yo, Tommy, I just shot Apple Head a block from the spot. Bullet ran off so I'm riding around looking for him right now," I explained, my heart racing.

"What do you mean, you shot him?" Tommy Boy wanted to know.

"I ran up on both of them, started asking Bullet questions about something he said about my niece Khloé, he denied it, so I looked at Apple Head and asked him to repeat what Bullet said, and he told me he wasn't telling me shit 'cause he wasn't a snitch. Then he turned his back on me and started walking away. So I asked that little nigga where he was going, and he ignored me. So I warned him and told him that he better turn around and face me, but he kept walking away, and I pulled my burner out and put three shots in his head."

"Did anybody see you?" Tommy Boy's questions continued.

"I don't know. I did not look around. All I did was look back to see where Bullet ran off to."

"Try to find Bullet and bring him to the spot. If you can't find him, then call me back."

"A'ight," I said, and then I hung up.

I swear, I drove up and down the five-block radius that covered our territory and I could not find that dude nowhere. Every corner I ran up on and saw my little leaders, I asked them had they seen him and everybody said no. Which led me to believe that he was in someone's house in this neighborhood. Three minutes into my search, I got a phone call from Jamie. I started not to answer it, but then I figured that he might be with Bullet.

"Yo, what's up?" he said.

"I'm in the neighborhood, why?"

"The cops and the ambulance are on the next block over. And a couple of dudes said that Apple Head is dead."

"Yeah, I already know."

"Do you know who did it?"

"I'll talk to you about that later. I'm out here looking for Bullet, so if you see him, let me know."

I did not give Jamie a chance to respond. I just disconnected our call because I had bigger fish to fry.

14

BAD COPS—KHLOÉ

After getting this high-tech video camera, I decided that it was time to test it out, and what better way than by doing my surveillance work on four dirty-ass cops. A couple of minutes into my drive, I decided to call my uncle Ed to keep him abreast on my whereabouts, just in case something happened to me. I knew that he would blame himself.

Once I dialed his number, his cell phone rang twice before he answered it. "Hey, Khloé, I'm gonna have to call you back." He sounded winded and distraught.

"What's going on? Are you okay?" I pressed him.

"Yeah, I'm good. Just let me call you back in a couple hours."

"All right, as soon as you get a chance, call me back," I urged him.

"A'ight," he said, and then my phone line went dead.

Kind of thrown off by my uncle talking to me like that, I wanted to call him back and see if I could squeeze it out of him, but I knew my uncle—he wouldn't fold under pressure, so I knew that I'd be wasting my time.

To sum up my agenda today, I figured that it would be a good idea to pay Brad Ford a visit at his place. Try to get a few photos of his wife. Maybe a couple photos of his kids too. Anything I could use as a pawn when everything was all said and done.

It did not take me long to pull up on his block in his cozy neighborhood. It was close to noon, so there were fewer cars parked in his neighbor's driveway. This was the perfect setup for me. So I pulled my car over to the side of the curb and turned off the ignition. I leaned my seat back enough so that I would not be seen if someone walked or drove by me. Armed with my high-tech video camera, I lay there with so many thoughts circling around in my head. One part of me had my heart pumping because I loved investigating people and situations. But then the other part of me made me feel like this wasn't just a normal investigation. Something about this whole thing was not adding up to me. Something was off. I couldn't quite put my finger on it, but I would, sooner rather than later.

Finally, after sitting in my freaking car for close to two hours, watching cars coming and going, birds flying around in the air, two female senior citizens power-walking, and the mailman doing his route, I got some movement from Brad. He hopped in his vehicle and drove by me like he was in a rush. This piqued my interest. It even got my heart and adrenaline pumping.

Immediately after he drove by me, he took a right turn onto the next block. Thankfully, no one was around when I powered up my car and sped after Brad. When I got to the corner, I saw that his vehicle was two blocks ahead of me. "Will you please slow your damn car down," I mumbled. I mean, there is a speed limit for residential streets. I bet if I were speeding that damn fast, there would be a cop posted somewhere around here just waiting to give my ass a speeding ticket. So much for street justice.

"Man, slow your ass down," I griped as I followed Brad.

But he was not letting up. He drove at a speed of forty-five miles per hour until he got on the nearby highway. That was where his speeding intensified. He went from forty-five to seventy miles per hour. The only upside to this was that on the highway everyone speeds, so this meant that I would blend in perfectly.

"Where are you going?" I uttered quietly as I tailed him from three or four cars behind. Curious and feeling on high alert, I wracked my brain trying to figure out where this guy was going. I followed him to the city of Chesapeake. According to my odometer, we traveled a total of fifteen miles. After we got off on the exit to Battlefield Boulevard, we took that street all the way down to Volvo Parkway. After five more left turns and two rights, we ended up in the deserted parking lot of a closed movie theater. Since I couldn't follow him all the way into the parking lot, I parked my car across the street from a Harris Teeter supermarket. I figured this was the perfect spot to use my new camera because my car blended in with all the shoppers at this grocery store. So, after I powered up my high-tech device, I zoomed in where Brad was and waited to see what was going to happen next.

Several minutes after Brad parked his vehicle in the abandoned parking lot, another car joined him. The car was a silver late-model Dodge Ram. And when the driver got out of the vehicle, I realized instantly that it was one of his cop buddies, Ryan Lopez. Ryan got out of his vehicle and got into Brad's, and sat there.

Brad's windows were 5 percent tinted, so having this video came in handy, otherwise I would be screwed. I couldn't hear what they were saying, but the zoom lens was a good trade-off. Now, what baffled me was why had the two come here to have a meeting? They could have waited until they got to work later to chat. Not even five minutes after both cops met up with each other, another vehicle pulled up. In fact, it was a black Cadillac Escalade, tricked out with tinted windows and chromed out with twenty-inch rims.

Only seconds after the driver parked his SUV, Brad and Ryan got out of their vehicle and the driver got out of his. All three men walked to the back of the Cadillac truck. They said a few words while the driver of the truck opened the lift. For the first couple of minutes I couldn't see the driver's face, but as soon as he grabbed a small, black dust bag from the back of this SUV, I realized that he was a known drug dealer from the area, by the name of Caesar. There was a lot of speculating that he was a sex trafficker as well. But no one had come forward to back that claim. Caesar was tall, but he had a slim build. But don't let his body frame fool you. He was linked to the murders of a lot of people. Men and women. But had never been charged and convicted. Now seeing him with two narcotics detectives, I knew why.

After he gave Brad the black dust bag, Brad pulled out the contents from it and for a brief second, I saw a stack of one-hundred-dollar bills wrapped in rubber bands. My guess was that it could easily be ten thousand dollars. Maybe more.

While Brad stuffed the money back into the dust bag, Caesar and Ryan started a dialogue. At one point, the conversation seemed humorous because Brad, Ryan, and Caesar laughed at one another. If I could only hear what they were saying, because whatever it was, it would have been icing on the cake.

All three losers huddled around each other for a total of eleven minutes. When their meeting was over, Caesar got back into his vehicle and left the scene while Brad and Ryan stayed behind. Brad and Ryan exchanged words and then they divvied up the money, shook each other's hands, and then they parted ways.

I sat in my car with the videocam in my hand and beamed with excitement that I had footage of crooked cops taking money from a known drug dealer. All three of those guys stood there and acted like they were best buddies. I knew that there was a lot of police corruption within the system, but to have evidence of their wrongdoings was like hitting the lottery. Now I knew Frances was gonna want an update about today's venture, so I was gonna have to figure out what to tell her without giving her all the dirt I had on Brad and his comrades.

After stumbling on all of this incriminating evidence, I figured that it wouldn't hurt me if I took the rest of the day off. Besides, I needed to lay out everything that I had so I could stay on course with the deadline I was given. *Who knows, I might be a great private investigator after all.*

En route to my apartment, I stopped by McDonald's and picked up a fish sandwich and a small fries. By the time I got home, my fries were gone, and my fish sandwich was half eaten. It sure hit the spot, because when I walked into my apartment, I realized how tired I was after I dropped my purse on the coffee table and collapsed on my sofa. I managed to use what energy I had left to grab the remote control and power on the TV. It was early in the afternoon, so I decided to watch a little bit of local news. Watching the news was something I did on the regular, considering I had been a journalist. I loved critiquing other news reporters' reporting tactics. Every news anchor competed with each other. Having the spotlight means that you are the best. The cream of the crop. Now I can say that I accomplished it, and it felt good.

The food I ate prior to my coming home really did a number on me, because I did not realize that I had fallen asleep until I heard a knock on my door. Somewhat startled, I sat up and looked at the time on my cable box. It read six forty-five, so I rose from the sofa and walked to the front door. "Who is it?" I shouted, while scratching my head.

"It's your uncle Ed," he responded.

Without saying another word, I opened the door and let him in. "There's been a slight change of plans," he said as he entered my apartment.

"What do you mean, there's been a slight change of plans?"

"I shot and killed this little dude earlier," he started off saying after he took a seat on my sofa.

I stood in the middle of the floor, trying to gather my thoughts. "Who. Did you shoot and kill?" I asked him. I needed some answers and I needed them now.

"Maggie's son Jamie told me that this new dude that just got initiated in our gang was talking shit about you. So I went to our spot at Park Place to confront him, but he wasn't there. Tommy Boy was there, so I asked him where was home boy at, and he told me that the little dude walked up the street to the corner store. After Tommy Boy told me where the dude was, I hopped in my car and headed towards the store. Halfway there I saw the little kid and another gang member named Apple Head walking in my direction, so I pulled my car over and told the little kid to come here. The other dude, Apple Head, came with him. After they both walked up to me, I asked the little kid to repeat to me what he said about you, but he suddenly got amnesia. So I asked Apple Head what the other kid had said, since he was in the room with him, and he told me that he ain't no rat and then he walked away from me. So I told him to bring his ass back to me, but he kept walking. Now being the OG of the organization, you are not supposed to walk away when I ask you a question. That is a form of disrespect on all levels. And then to do it in front of someone else, is a no-no."

"So, what happened? Was he the one you shot and killed?"

"Yeah, I couldn't just let him walk away and ignore me. What kind of message would I be sending if I would have allowed him to walk away from me like that? No one in our crew would respect me." He pleaded his case.

"Did anyone see you?"

"I don't know."

"What about the other guy? What did you do to him?"

"I didn't do shit to him. As soon as I shot the other guy, he ran off in the opposite direction."

"Do you know where he is?"

"Nah, me and some of the other soldiers went on a manhunt and we can't pinpoint where he went to."

"What did the OGs have to say? Are they mad about what happened?"

"Nah, not really. I mean, their only issue was why I did it near the spot. Not only that, they just told me that the dude I murdered and the one that ran off were cousins."

I took a seat beside him and put my arm around his neck. "No way. So, what are you going to do now?" I wanted to know.

"I don't know. I do know that I'm gonna stay away from the spot in Park Place for a while until this shit blows over. Other than that, I don't know."

"Think the other little kid is going to snitch on you? Go to the cops and tell them what happened?"

"I'm not sure. We just recruited him. So he's new. I mean, who knows. He may ride for his family instead of our brotherhood. But I do know that if he does rat me out, he's dead, because the prosecutors ain't gonna protect him. All the prosecutor wants is a conviction, and once they get that, homeboy is on his own. Everybody will find out that he's a snitch and kill him on sight. Even the other gangs will kill him on sight. That's just how the streets work."

"Does Maggie know about this?"

"Yeah, I just left home. I told her everything."

"What did she say?"

"She's upset because now she believes that I'm gonna have to look over my shoulder."

"She's right, Unc."

"Look, you know me, and I ain't afraid to get locked up. That shit doesn't bother me. My only reason for coming over here and talking to you in person is because I don't want to take any chances of being with you and the cops run up on me. Remember, the dude does know that you are my niece. Him talking shit about you is why I stepped to him in the first place."

"Damn, so that means that you can't be my night escort!" I whined, pouting like a little kid while trying to wrap all this shit around my mind.

"I know, I know. But this is for the best, Khloé. You got a job to do and I'm gonna be a major distraction if cops see me and you together," he tried to explain. And the more he talked, the more I understood where he was coming from.

"So, what are you going to do, moving forward? Stay low-key? Stay in the house?"

"Yeah, for a few days."

"Who at the spot knows where you live?"

"Some of the older members. The nigga I shot, and his cousin, didn't know."

"Think the other ones will rat you out?"

"Nah, those niggas would take a bullet for me. We're a tight unit."

"Okay, well, as long as you know who you're around, I guess you'll be all right," I started off saying, and then I rubbed my uncle Eddie on his knee. "If I lose you, I don't know what I'll do. So, will you please lay low?"

He smiled at me and said, "I'll try."

We talked a little bit more about his situation and how he planned to stay a couple steps ahead of the homicide detectives if they found out he was involved. Then we shifted the conversation to the surveillance footage I got earlier today. I grabbed the video camera and showed him what I had to work with.

"Look at the pictures and video I got today," I said, and started flicking through the pictures I had on the camera.

My uncle zoomed in as I sifted through each photo.

"You know who this is, right?" I pointed towards the guy named Caesar. He was handing Brad the black dust bag with the money in it.

"Yeah everybody knows who he is."

"Think you can guess how much money he had in his hands?"

"No, but the stacks looked really fat."

"Well, it looks like fifteen- or twenty-thousand dollars to me."

"Yeah, it looks like that amount to me too."

"Can you tell me why Caesar gave that cop that much money?"

"I can name two reasons."

"What are they?"

"Caesar is buying his time on the streets. And he could be giving that cop profit money too."

"What do you mean, profit money?"

"When narcotics cops bust in stash houses, they take the drugs and then they sell it to a dealer on the streets. That's common practice. So, in this picture it looks like the cop had already fronted Caesar the drugs and now he's paying the cop back."

"Uncle Eddie, why do you think the other two cops aren't with them? Why were these two alone?"

"Probably because they didn't want to split it up four ways."

"Okay, that makes sense."

"So, what are you going to do with these pics and video?"

"I haven't quite mapped it out yet, but I'll figure it out, especially since now I gotta do this whole investigation by myself. You so hotheaded. As soon as somebody says something about me, you are ready to kill them."

"You damn right. I won't let no one disrespect you. Two of the bullets I put in Apple Head were supposed to be for the other guy. But he ran off."

"Uncle Eddie, can you please stay out of trouble?"

"Yeah, I'll try my best," he replied. "So, whatcha got planned for the rest of the day?"

"I was invited to a dinner party tomorrow, so I'm going home and take all night to find something really nice to wear."

"Sounds like fun."

"I need some to take my mind off everything."

"I'm sure that they may do the trick."

I guess I will find out sooner than later."

Saying yes to this dinner party tomorrow night wasn't a bad choice after all. I mean, look what happened with my uncle. He now had to stay off the radar because of that shit he just put himself in. While I sorted through my collection of evening wear, I got a phone call from Liza, my old news station colleague. I answered her call on the second ring. "Hey, stranger, what's up?" I said.

"How are you?" she asked.

"I'm good—and you?"

"You know me. It's always work, work, work. And speaking of which, there was a shooting today in Park Place. Heard anything about it? Has any names been circulating? Gang related or what?"

"Yes, I saw it on the news, but I haven't heard any names circulating though," I lied. And she knew it too. She knows that I am well connected in the streets, especially since I'm from the streets.

"Bullshit! You know something!" She chuckled. "If you don't know who actually pulled the trigger, you know someone that knows someone that's involved." She pressed me.

I tried to reason with her. "I swear, if I knew I would tell you in a heartbeat. I mean, what good would that information do for me? I can't use it. I'm no longer a journalist."

"Khloé, please don't lie to me," Liza begged.

"Liza, I'm not lying to you. But I'll tell you what, I'm gonna ask around and as soon as I hear something, I will call you," I assured her.

"Promise?"

"Yes, I promise."

15

THIS IS MY TOWN—UNCLE ED

When I arrived home, Jamie was sitting at the kitchen table eating a slice of pizza with Maggie, who was sitting next to him. I heard them mumbling something, but I could not make out what they were saying.

Maggie started up the dialogue. "Back so soon?"

"Yep," I replied as I grabbed a bottle of Corona from the refrigerator. After I took the top off, I drank a mouthful and savored the taste and coldness that slowly went down my throat.

"Did you tell Khloé what happened?" Maggie wanted to know.

"Yeah, I just left her apartment," I answered while looking at Jamie's body language. He was eating a slice of pizza, but he acted like he wasn't enjoying it. Maybe he wasn't enjoying it because I was in his space.

"What did she say?" Maggie pressed the issue.

"Not much. Just that she didn't want me walking around here looking over my shoulder."

"That's it," Maggie said. She was getting aggravated. "You left this house to go and confront a guy that talked shit about her, shot and killed someone else, and that's all she had to say?"

"Look, she was upset too. What else do you want me to say?" I asked after I took another sip of beer.

"That's still not enough. Do you know that the streets are talking?" Maggie blurted out. She said it like she could not contain herself.

"Do you think that I care about what the streets are saying? I am my own man. I have taken care of myself all these fucking years, so don't sit there and act like you're warning me. You know that I'm not afraid of anyone walking on two feet."

"A couple of the guys at the spot found out that I told you what Bullet said about your niece, and now when I walk into a room, it gets quiet. Or everybody leaves the room," Jamie interjected as he chewed on a slice of pizza.

"Jamie, check it out. Now, I'm sorry that everybody at the spot is looking at you like a snitch, but they're not our real family. We're a brotherhood. If something jumps off in the street, we look out for one another. But Khloé is blood family, and she comes first before any of those dudes on Thirty-First Street." I took another sip of beer from my bottle of Corona.

"Nah, dude, she ain't my family, she's your family," Jamie disagreed. "Your niece wouldn't die for me, but those dudes on Thirty-First and Thirty-Second would do it, so let's get it straight," he continued, the pitch of his voice getting higher.

"Yo, Jamie, you better calm your ass down. I know that you're grown now, and you think that you're a man, but I'm a man too and this is my table you're sitting at, so get it together," I reminded him.

Jamie stood from the table like he was about to stand toe to toe with me, but he did not move one inch.

"So, whatcha gonna do, step to me like a man?" I asked him.

"Nah, I ain't gotta step to you, because you already know what it is. All I gotta say is that this may be your kitchen table, but this is my mama's house," he said, and then he left the room.

"Don't run now, nigga!" I shouted. After Maggie heard Jamie walk out the front door, she looked at me like she was truly disappointed. "You really being extra right now," she commented.

"No, he was being extra talking about Khloé isn't family."

"But she's not. Not to him, anyway."

"Oh, so you're riding with him on this, huh?"

"Eddie, do you realize that you left out of here to go and kill somebody?"

"You act like I meant to do that. I just wanted to talk to the little dude about what he said and straighten him out. You know, make him apologize. That's it."

"But that's not what happened."

"Damn, how many times are you going to remind me of that shit?"

"Until it sinks into your head."

"Well, you ain't gotta do that. I know what I did wrong. And I can't change that," I said, and then I placed the empty bottle of beer on the countertop next to me. "What was y'all talking about before I came in the house?" I continued.

"The same thing he told you about the members looking at him differently now, and how a couple of them walked out the game room when he walked in there."

"They shouldn't have done that. I'm gonna have a talk with Tommy Boy so that shit don't happen again."

"But he doesn't want you to do that. You running to

Tommy Boy and telling him what the guys are doing to Jamie isn't gonna do anything but make the situation worse. He doesn't want you to talk to anyone. Just let him handle it on his own."

"All right," I said, finally agreeing to let that situation work itself out.

"So, where do we go from here?" Maggie steered the conversation away from Jamie.

"I really don't know."

"Are you going to keep your word and stay away from the spot until the dust settles?"

"Yeah, I'm gonna let things cool off."

"What are you going to do if that guy gives you up to the cops?"

"Come on, Maggie, you already know what's gonna happen. What, ya need me to say it on the record or something?" I replied sarcastically.

"Ed, don't play with me," she responded, and then she got up from the table to leave the kitchen. I grabbed her arm before she made an exit.

"Where are you going?"

"Ed, let my arm go."

"I'll let you go if you don't leave the kitchen." I tried to compromise with her.

"Let me go, Ed."

"Not until you tell me that you ain't leaving."

"I'm only going in the living room."

"Okay, well, I'm going with you," I said, and we moved into the living room. She took a seat on the end of the sofa and I took a seat next to her.

"You are really getting on my nerves right now."

Before I could say something, someone knocked on the front door. "Who is it?" Maggie shouted towards the front door.

"It's Detective Lewis and Detective Myers from the homicide unit."

The fact that two fucking cops from homicide were at my front door made me jump up on my feet. I was in semi-paranoid mode. Maggie shot a look at me. I saw fear in her eyes. And I could tell that she had no idea what to do next. I grabbed her and pulled her up on her feet. "I'm going in the bedroom. And I don't care what they say, they cannot come into this house without a search warrant, okay?"

"Okay," she said.

While Maggie headed to the front door, I sprinted down the hallway, went into our bedroom, and then I hid inside the walk-in closet.

Seconds later, Maggie opened the door. "How can I help you?" I heard her say.

"We're looking for Eddie, is he here?" I heard the cop reply.

"Are you sure you got the right house, because I don't know an Eddie," Maggie told him.

"Ma'am, the kids that are playing downstairs in the parking lot said that he lives here. So please, don't waste our time," I heard a woman's voice say.

"You're actually wasting my time."

"Okay, Myers, let me handle this," I heard the guy cop say.

"Yes, let him handle this because you're barking up the wrong tree." Maggie didn't let up.

"I'm sorry, ma'am, but what is your name?" the guy cop asked.

"You should already know that. 'Cause whoever told you to come here, had to have given you my name."

"Ma'am, just tell us where Eddie is, because if you keep screwing with us, we will lock you up for harboring a murder suspect!" the female cop roared. I could tell that she was livid. But never mind her, did she just say that I was a murder suspect? Hearing those words made my heart drop into the pit of my stomach.

"Look, police lady, that shit you just said did not faze me. Now, step back before I slam my door in your face," Maggie warned her.

"Here you go, ma'am. Take my card, and if you happen to see Eddie, give him my card or give him my number and tell him to call me. We just wanna ask him a few questions," the male cop said.

"I told you that I don't know him. Stop. Don't come here and knock on my door no more," Maggie spat, and then I heard the front door slam.

As bad as I wanted to walk out of this closet, I felt that it was better if Maggie came to me first. Having the cops knocking on my front door threw me off course a little. I mean, how the fuck did word get around that damn fast? Did that little nigga Bullet really snitch on me about killing his cousin? If he did, then he's one dead nigga.

"I know you heard what I said to both of those cops," she stated after she opened the closet door.

"Yeah, I heard everything," I told her as I exited the closet. I walked over to the bed and took a seat on the edge of it.

"Sounds like that little guy told them that you killed his cousin," Maggie insisted.

"Yeah, I think you might be right," I said reluctantly.

"So, what are we going to do now? Someone told them that you live here, so they're coming back. They might even put a couple of cops outside to watch the house," Maggie suggested.

"I thought about that too, especially since the kids outside told them that I live here."

"You're gonna have to lay low. If you need anything, I'm gonna have to leave the house and get it for you."

"Maggie, I'm my own man. You don't have to do that."

"Just be quiet and listen. You always have to have the last word."

"What do you want me to say?"

"I don't want you to say anything. Let me get in the driver's seat for once. I need you out here on the streets with me. Not locked up behind bars, sharing a cell with another nigga with a life sentence."

"Yeah, a'ight," I said, because Maggie was right. Just this once, let her run the show and who knows, I might just get out of this situation.

After settling down in the bedroom, I think an hour passed and then someone knocked on the front door. I froze for a second and then I jumped up from the bed as my heart rate soared. Maggie rushed down the hallway and entered our bedroom to see where I was. I was standing next to the closet, just in case I had to go back in hiding.

"Who's at the front door?" I asked her, my voice barely audible.

"I don't know. I ran back here first before I opened the door. Do you want me to answer it?" Maggie whispered.

"Think it could be Jamie?"

"No, remember Jamie has a key."

"Oh yeah,"

"Think it could be the cops again?"

"Nah, they wouldn't do that. They know that you could get them in trouble for harassment."

"Well, whoever it is, they'll get the message and go on about their business," Maggie insisted, and then she walked away from me. She left the bedroom and started walking down the hallway, taking light steps as though if she walked any louder, she would be heard from the other side of the front door.

While watching Maggie tiptoe back down the hallway, all I could think about was where my life would go from here. Being stuck in this confined space was going to run me crazy. Now, I knew that a jail cell was even smaller, but I did not have a choice in that matter. But now, I did. Whoever was at the front door left after knocking seven times and realizing that no one was going to answer. Now, all they had to do was stay away totally.

An hour later Jamie walked back in the house. I was still in the bedroom, but I was watching the movie *Training Day* starring my dude Denzel Washington. "Ma, whatcha cooking?" I heard him say. The other thing I heard was his footsteps on the plastic liner on the floor of the hallway.

"I'm gonna make a pot of chicken and dumplings," she replied.

"Cool," he replied, and then I heard the bathroom door close.

I got up from the bed and made my way into the kitchen. I wanted to be in the same room with Maggie when I got her to ask him if he was around when someone knocked on the front door after he left. While Jamie was in the bathroom, I got Maggie's ear and instructed her to ask him where he was after he walked out of the house earlier. It seemed like as soon as I convinced her to do it, Jamie had already walked back out of the bathroom and into the kitchen. I pretended to be looking in the pot of chicken she was boiling.

"When is that going to be done?" Jamie asked her. "Because I'm hungry." He tried to avoid eye contact with me, so that's when I knew that he was still upset about how things went before he stormed out the house earlier.

"In about another forty-five minutes." As soon as she answered his question, I headed back out of the kitchen and went into the living room. I wanted to give him his space while he was in the kitchen with Maggie. I've learned over the years how sons are very territorial when it comes to spending time with their mothers. I was like that with my mother as well.

Maggie started questioning him. "Where did you go after you left out of here earlier?"

"I went to Lily's crib, why?" he answered.

"Did you see the cops knocking on my door while you were at Lily's place?"

"Wait, the police was here?"

"Yeah, you didn't see them?"

"Nah," he started off saying. "When Lily let me into her crib, we went straight to her bedroom."

Hearing this little dude tell me that he took Lily to her bedroom after she let him into her house was like a blow to my ego. I don't know if he suspected that I fucked Lily before, or had an idea that I did, but either way, he sure knew how to throw that shit in my face at times when I wasn't in the mood to hear it.

"Jamie, are you sure you didn't see the cops come here?" Maggie pressed him.

"No, Ma, I didn't. When did they come here?"

"A few minutes after you left."

"What did they want?"

I spoke up. "They came here looking for me."

By this time, Jamie was standing by the entryway of the kitchen and living room so he could see me clearly. "What did they want?" he asked me after turning his focus towards me.

"They told your mama that they wanted to talk to me about a murder. But she told 'em that I didn't live here, and she didn't know me."

"Mama, what did they say when you told them that?" Jamie asked after he turned his focus towards Maggie.

"Well, apparently they didn't believe me because one of them handed me their business card. And then I closed my front door."

"Think it's about Apple Head?" Jamie asked me. He looked generally concerned.

"It can't be about anything else. I mean, what else could they come here for?" I tried to reason.

Jamie pressed the issue. "Think somebody ratted you out?"

"Of course they did. Why else would the cops come here looking for me?"

"Think it was Bullet? Because no one has seen him since what happened earlier."

"Now I do," I said.

Jamie looked down at the floor and then he looked back at me. "I know that we don't get along all the time, but I know that my mom loves you, and if you go to prison that would hurt my mom. So I'm gonna go round my dudes up and handle that situation," Jamie said.

I swear, hearing this little guy tell me how much it would bother him to see Maggie hurt if I got locked up meant a lot to me. It meant a lot to Maggie too. She walked over from the stove and put her arms around him. "Awwww . . . I love you so much, Jamie," she said as she overloaded him with kisses all over his face.

"Good looking-out, Jamie, I truly appreciate it," I told him.

Maggie was in the bedroom when she got a call, so she walked back in the living room with her cell phone in her hand. She held it out for me to take it. "Who is it?" I asked her.

"It's Jamie," she replied.

"What's up?" I said immediately after I took the phone from her hand.

"We've been beating these streets up looking for that dude, and he's ghosted. We even went by his mom's crib and nobody answered the door. She's a dope fiend, so she could be anywhere."

"What about Apple Head's peoples? Think he might be there?"

"Apple Head's mom was murked last year by her boyfriend for cheating on him. He killed the dude that she was cheating with too."

"What about his pops?"

"He locked up doing a life."

"What about a grandma? Or an auntie?" I suggested. I was grasping at straws at this point.

"If he's got one, they don't live around here."

"Damn, that's bullshit!" I commented as I gritted my teeth. "A'ight, well, keep your eyes open, and if something comes up let me know."

"A'ight," Jamie said and our call ended.

I placed Maggie's cell phone on the coffee table in front of us. She started rubbing my back in a circular motion. She does this to me to remind me that she has my back. More times than not, it works, but in this moment, it didn't. Like I said before, I wasn't afraid of anyone walking on two feet. But at this point, I didn't wanna go back to prison and leave Maggie out here alone. She's a great woman, and I wanted to spend the rest of my life with her, not behind bars. Now, if I didn't have a woman in my life, I would say, *Catch me if you can* . . .

"What did he say?" she inquired.

"He said that him and his boys been searching the streets, but they can't find Bullet nowhere. He said that they been to his mom's crib and to Apple Head's mom's crib, and nobody was there. So I told him to keep looking."

"I sure hope they find him. Because until they do, he will have your life in his hands," Maggie expressed, and she was right, that nigga Bullet had my freedom in his hands. And it didn't feel good either.

I devoured a bowl of chicken and dumplings after Maggie placed a huge bowl of it in front of me. To wash it down, I drank an ice-cold Pepsi and then I retired to the living room. While watching reruns of *Good Times*, I heard a knock on the front door. Maggie was in the bedroom, so I got up from the sofa and quietly made my way down the hallway. We passed each other when I entered in the bedroom.

"Who is it?" she whispered.

"I don't know," I said and headed for the bedroom closet.

"*Who is it?*" Maggie shouted.

"It's me, Lily. Girl, come open this door," I heard Lily say.

I swear, it was a relief knowing that it was Lily and not the cops. Instead of going back in the living room, I climbed on the bed and closed the bedroom door slightly. I left it open just enough so that I could hear what was going on but I couldn't be seen.

"I came over here because my kids said that two police officers knocked on your door earlier," Lily started off saying.

"Yeah, they came here asking for some guy named Neal. I told them I didn't know a guy name Neal. So they left," Maggie replied. What she said was a lie. But to hear her keep Lily out of our business was genius on her part.

"You know me and your son is getting married," Lily said, keeping the conversation flowing.

I heard Maggie chuckle. "Girl, stop kidding yourself. My son ain't marrying nobody."

"Yes, he is. He told me when he came over to my apartment earlier."

"He says that to everybody so he can sleep with them."

"But I'm different."

"Don't get your hopes high."

"Anyway, whatever, where's your hubby?"

"Who, Ed?"

"Yeah."

"In the bedroom, I think."

"I wonder if he heard about some dude getting shot out at Park Place earlier?" I heard Lily say. I swear, hearing her utter the words *getting shot* and *Park Place* sent a sharp pain in my side. I mean, what was her angle? Was she here to update us about matters of the street, or was she here to fish for answers? Either way, I wasn't feeling it.

"Jamie said something to us about it. But other than that, it's been quiet."

"But the guy that got shot was in Eddie's gang, Ace of Spades." Lily pressed the issue.

Now at that very moment, I wanted to go to the front of the apartment and snap her fucking neck because she wouldn't shut her freaking mouth. Maggie just expressed to her that we heard about it, but that's it. That topic stays there, so leave it there.

"I don't think so, because someone would've called Ed by now."

"Well, that ain't what I heard," Lily insisted.

I wasn't feeling this conversation at all. If Maggie wasn't here and I knew for certain that the cops weren't outside watching this apartment, I would drag Lily's ass out of this house by her hair and tell her to get a fucking life. She's so damn messy. I'm so mad that I fucked her. Doing it was a bad judgment call on my part.

"Girl, hush up about that mess. Let the guy's family deal with that."

"Wait, don't shoot the messenger."

"I will if you say something else about that guy."

Maggie said a few more words to Lily and then she escorted her out of our apartment. I was happy to hear that that tramp left, because if I had to tell her, then it probably wouldn't have gone well. That's that street shit that's imbedded inside of me.

16

THE FOLLOWING DAY—KHLOÉ

After running around all day, doing stakeouts and surveillance work, I headed home to get ready because the dinner party event was finally here. I found the perfect little dark blue formfitting dress with a low neckline and low-back design, a pair of Jimmy Choo stilettos, and to set things in the right direction I carried a silver Prada clutch. Knowing how sexy I looked, I knew that I was going to turn heads at the party.

After I pulled up in front of this gorgeous, colonial-style home, I was greeted by a valet driver. When he opened my car door, he handed me a ticket and then he got into my car. In total, there were five valet drivers prioritizing everyone's car as they drove up. As I entered the two large double doors, I was greeted by a server and was handed a glass of champagne. "Thank you," I said after I took the glass in my hand.

I took a sip of the champagne and moved into the room. It was colossal. The floors were white marble with columns neatly placed in four sections of the floor. In the left side of the room was a four-man orchestra. The music they were playing was beautiful and angelic. To the left of the orchestra were partygoers, sipping on their alcoholic beverages while chatting to the people around them. As I continued to walk farther into the room, I spotted Taylor speaking with the mayor of the city, so I headed in her direction. I wanted her to know that I had arrived.

I had to walk by ten people to get to Taylor, and when I tapped on her shoulder, she turned around and faced me with the biggest smile she could muster up and then she embraced me. "Oh my God! You made it. Thank you so much for coming," she said.

"Thank you for the invite."

"You're welcome," she added. "I see you have a drink, so enjoy it while I introduce you to the mayor of our town, Arnold Blackwood."

I turned around, faced the mayor, and shook his hand. "Nice to meet you. My name is Khloé Mercer."

"No need to introduce yourself. I know who you are," he replied. Arnold Blackwood was just elected mayor six months ago. He was a chubby Black man with a bad taste in attire. He kind of reminded me of Eddie Murphy's huge character in the movie called *Nutty Professor II: The Klumps*. His taste in cologne was even worse. He smelled like he was some bad oil from a street vendor. And as much as I didn't want to shake his hand, I did it because he extended his hand.

"Don't say that, you're making me blush," I said while I shook his hand.

"You did an awesome job a couple of weeks ago when you helped crack open that murder case," he told me.

"Trust me, I didn't do it alone. We have some very talented journalists at the news network."

"I'm sure you do, but you are the one that shined," he added.

"Hey, darling, come and meet my high school friend Khloé Mercer," Taylor said after she pulled her husband from talking to someone behind us. When he turned around, our eyes met. Taylor's husband was a very handsome guy. But he was a very short guy. I remember seeing his face on everybody's lawn in front of their house. In his online debate, he promised to help cut taxes and pay the school teachers a better salary, but just like other politicians, we have yet to see it.

"Nice to meet you, Khloé. I've heard so much about you these last couple days. Not like I didn't know who you are in the first place, but to know that my wife knows you is cool."

I smiled. "She was the popular one in school," I stated.

"Yeah, but you were best dressed," Taylor insisted.

"This is a beautiful party," I complimented them.

"Thank you," her husband said. "And our bill will reflect that." He chuckled.

I chuckled while the mayor said, "Our wives definitely know how to spend money, huh?" He directed the comment to Taylor's husband.

"And on that note, I'm gonna go and mingle with Bob, our city counsel," Taylor's husband joked as he scooted away from our circle.

"You are not leaving me," the mayor announced in a joking manner, and then he scooted away too.

"See how they start things and then leave the kitchen when those things get hot?" Taylor teased as she grabbed the hem of his suit jacket before he got out of arm's reach. "Anyway, let's go and meet some more people," she insisted as she grabbed hold of my hand and pulled me in the opposite direction.

I had only been at this party for a little over thirty minutes and Farrah had introduced me to everyone that had clout in the city of Norfolk. And what's bizarre is that everyone I spoke to knew who I was at first glance. I literally felt like a local celebrity. After four glasses of champagne and two cocktails, I was buzzing and it felt good. It had been a year since I got toasted like this. I mean, it wasn't a bad thing, because I was enjoying myself. Spending this little bit of time in this atmosphere felt rewarding. It was even encouraging me to hang out more. Socialize some. I knew one thing: After I finished this case, I was going on vacation. Go to Hawaii and spend a week there, soaking up the sun and eating some great food. I couldn't wait.

"Taylor, where is the restroom?" I asked after following her around the party for at least an hour.

"Let me show you," she offered. She led me around two corners and then she walked me to the restroom door. "Here it is," she announced. "I'll be back in the reception area when you're done."

"Okay, see you in a minute," I told her.

Thankfully, the bathroom was empty when I walked inside because I hate sharing bathrooms with other people. Most of them are inconsiderate when it comes to flushing the toilets, and the sink area seems like it's always wet and messy looking. Now the only reason why I asked Taylor to use her bathroom was because this house was her home. In addition to that, there was no way that she would have an unsanitary bathroom, especially while she was having this upscale event.

Like I suspected, Taylor's bathroom was in immaculate condition, and seeing this, I was in and out in a jiffy. I looked for Taylor as soon as I left the bathroom and found her talking to her husband. I approached them. "I'm back," I said cheerfully. At that same time, another couple stepped up to the circle Taylor, her husband, and myself, had created.

"Hey, dude, glad you could make it," Taylor's husband said.

I smiled because I love when people come together for a common goal.

Taylor introduced the couple to me. "Khloé, this is Kate Ford and that's her husband, Brad, who can't stop talking to my husband for a second."

I swear, a rush of heat engulfed me. It felt like I was about to be swallowed whole. I mean, who would've thought that I would meet the very person I was investigating for a client? This was unreal.

"Hi, nice to meet you," Kate said, and shook my hand.

Holding a glass that looked like it was filled up with vodka, Brad smiled and shook my hand as well. His felt very sweaty and I was immediately grossed out. After he let my hand go, he said, "You're that reporter that broke that homicide case, huh?" His words slurred a bit.

"I'm not taking credit for that. Your colleagues in the homicide division did that all on their own. I just reported when I was given information," I explained, while sobering up by the minute. Trust me, whatever buzz I had before I went in the bathroom, it was slipping away.

"I see we have a modest one on our hands," he commented, and then he took another sip from his glass.

"I think we do too," his wife agreed.

"Oh, leave my high school buddy alone. She's here to wind down and hopefully do a piece on this event we're having tonight," Taylor hinted as she nudged my arm.

"Oh, that would be really nice," Kate said. "Make sure you put me in there and tell everyone that I was nice," she added.

"No, put me in there," Brad interjected. "Tell all the people in the seven cities that my squad and I are beating these streets every day and arresting all the bad guys so that we can keep the streets safe and clean." He took another sip from his glass.

"Khloé, never mind him. He's only kidding," his wife said.

I smiled. But on the inside, I was about to fall apart. "It's cool," I finally said.

"Brad, let's get us another drink," Taylor's husband suggested after Brad emptied the contents of his glass.

Brad chuckled. "Thought that you'd never ask."

"Honey, don't drink too much," Kate warned him as he and Taylor's husband walked off.

"Oh, leave him alone. Let him have his fun. You are the designated driver, right?" Taylor reminded her.

"That's the thing. When I see him drinking, then I can't drink," Kate pointed out.

"She has a point there," I commented, while at the same time trying to deflect how I was really feeling. "Speaking of the word *point*, please point me back in the direction of the bathroom. I think I gotta use it again," I lied. I needed to get out of this place altogether.

"Go down that hallway and make a left turn," Taylor instructed me.

"Thank you," I replied and walked off. I headed in the direction she indicated, but as soon as she turned her back on me, I made a beeline towards the front door after I placed my half-filled glass on a tray one of the waiters was carrying.

Finally, I was outside, and a calm breeze hit me. I swear, the fresh air couldn't have felt better. "Can you bring my car around?" I told one of the valet drivers as I handed him my ticket.

"Sure," he said, and then he ran off.

While I stood there and waited for my car, I occasionally looked over my shoulders to see if I was being looked for by Taylor, or if Detective Brad Ford and his wife had a change of heart and decided that it was time to leave. Luckily for me, neither happened. "Here you go, ma'am," my valet driver said after he hopped out of my car. I tipped him five bucks, got in my car, and then I sped away.

I took a deep breath and exhaled. My nerves sort of calmed and my heart rate slowed down too. "What the fuck just happened?" I asked myself. But it was almost as if it was a whisper.

What were the odds of seeing that prick Brad Ford? And to see his wife with him. He was standing in a huddle with my old school buddy, acting like he didn't have a care in the world. All those people at Taylor's home looked at him as a hero. But I knew he was totally a different person. He was a monster. A fucking predator. I wonder how his wife would've reacted if she knew that fraud husband of hers is a thief, a rapist, and a drug-dealing bully? Would she be shocked? Or embarrassed? Or did she already know but carried on a façade that she and him were the poster folks for the American family.

While replaying my meeting and introduction to the narcotics Detective Brad Ford and his wife, my cell phone rang. I knew that it couldn't be anyone other than Frances, and I was right. "Hi, Frances," I greeted her.

"Hi, Khloé, how are you?" she replied.

"Well, I was invited out to a dinner party, so I went. Had a little bit of fun. Drinking a few cocktails, but then that all went down the drain. So now I'm on my way home."

"Oh great, you're out and about?"

"Yes, unfortunately."

"Cool, well, let's meet up for our daily update."

"Where would you like to meet?" I asked her. But I was not in the mood to see her tonight. I just wanted to go home so I could get my mind together.

"Let's meet up at the Taco Bell located on Northampton Boulevard," I suggested since it was only a couple miles away from my apartment and from where I was now.

"All right, I'll see you shortly."

Now my apartment was closer to this place than Frances's, but for some reason she got there faster than me. She was ready.

Three minutes and five stop lights later, I made it to Taco Bell. When I pulled into the parking lot, there was only two other cars there. And because of how empty the restaurant looked on the inside, I figured that the two cars belonged to the employees; in other words, it looked like a ghost town here. Thankfully I didn't have to wait long. A couple minutes later, Frances drove into the parking lot.

"Come and get in my car," I instructed her.

With ease, Frances got out of her vehicle and hopped into mine. "You look gorgeous," she complimented me.

"I don't feel gorgeous," I stated as I leaned back and grabbed the video camera that was on the floor behind the passenger seat.

"So, what happened at this event?"

"I thought I was going to this party to have a few cocktails and mingle a bit. So, the first part went off without a hitch, but then I turned around and was introduced to Brad Ford and his wife."

"Hey, wait, so you went to the dinner party hosted by a childhood friend tonight."

"Was it for the mayor?"

"Yes, it was."

"I know that whole circle of people."

"What a small world," I commented.

"Tell me about it. Because after seeing the cop and his wife there, I almost had a panic attack."

"Did he talk much?"

"He was too toasted to talk. He said *nice to meet you* and maybe something else. But for the most part, he had his glass up to his mouth."

"How did his wife act?"

"She was cool. Every time someone cracked a joke, she laughed. If only she knew that her husband is a scumbag. I betcha she wouldn't smile again."

"You're absolutely right. But to hell with them, show me what you have for me." Frances changed the subject. I leaned back and grabbed the video camera from the floor behind the passenger seat. When I had the video camera in hand, I gave it to her. She looked at it like it was a big piece of candy. She seemed anxious about what she was going to see.

She powered on the camera and that's when I instructed her to look at the photos of Brad getting a dust bag of money from a known drug dealer named Caesar. She didn't look surprised as she sifted through the photos and when she finished, she handed the camera back to me. "Is that it?"

"What do you mean, is that it? That's major right there. I got a narcotics detective taking a bag full of money from a drug dealer," I pointed out. I was appalled at her reaction. I mean, cops will kill whoever they have to if they find out that you have damaging evidence that could put them in prison and take away their pension.

"Khloé, I asked you to get me some evidence that would prove that they killed my husband. I don't give a damn about payoffs."

"So, how do you expect me to find evidence that they killed your husband? Those cops aren't walking around here killing other people and leaving a trail that I could follow. Those guys are involved in drugs and bribes. That's it," I tried to explain. This bitch was trying my patience. I mean, how dare she tell me that the work I was doing wasn't good enough. Was she crazy? Or was she sniffing coke?

"I paid you the money you asked me for, so I expect for you to deliver. I don't know how you're gonna do it. But I do know that I need it done ASAP. You have two more days."

"Look, will you at least take a look at the video?" I suggested. I knew the video footage was no different from the photos she saw, but I just wanted to show her that I had been working.

She watched the entire video and when it ended, she made it known that she was not impressed at all. And when she held out the video camera for me to take, she and I heard someone talking, so we sat there quietly. And that's when we realized that it was coming from the video camera. She turned the device around and looked down at the screen. I leaned over to look at it when I heard my voice. The screen of the camera was pointing down at the floor. The video camera focused in on my Uncle Eddie's shoes next.

"Caesar is buying his time on the streets. And he could be giving that cop profit money too," I heard my Uncle Eddie say.

"What do you mean, profit money?"

"When narcotics cops bust in stash houses, they take the drugs and then they sell it to a dealer on the streets. That's common practice. So, in this picture it looks like the cop had already fronted Caesar the drugs and now he's paying the cop back."

"Uncle Eddie, tell me why the other two cops aren't with them? Why were these two alone?"

"Probably because they didn't want to split up the money four ways."

"Okay, that makes sense."

"So, what are you going to do with these pics and video?"

"I haven't quite mapped it out yet, but I'll figure it out, especially since now I gotta do this whole investigation by myself. You so hotheaded. As soon as somebody says something about me, you are ready to kill them."

"You damn right. I won't let no one disrespect you. The two bullets I put in Apple Head was supposed to be for the other guy. But he ran off."

"Uncle Eddie, can you please stay out of trouble?"

"Yeah, I'll try my best," he replied.

When the recording ended, I wanted to shrivel up and disappear. Frances swayed her head around and gave me a hard stare. Then her stare turned into a grimace. She made me feel like I was in *The Twilight Zone*. "So, your uncle was the shooter in that young guy's murder, huh? And the fact that you know about it is icing on the cake," she said, but it was more like a trick question.

"That's not what my uncle and I are talking about," I lied, and grabbed the camera from her hands.

She disagreed. "Sounded like that to me. Looks like I've got me a few poker chips," she added. Her facial expression was wicked.

"Frances, don't play games with me. I don't care what you thought you heard. Just know that you can't go and bark up the wrong tree," I expressed to her, indirectly telling her that my uncle and the dudes he deals with would kill her on the spot if she tried to blackmail him.

"Believe me, I can go and bark up anyone's tree that I want. Now, you just do the job I paid you to do. And remember that you only have two days left until Friday comes," she said, and then she got out of my car.

I watched her get back in her car and drive away. I swear, I was in a moment where I wished that there was an explosive device underneath her car and I could've blown it up. *Nothing would make me happier than to see that bitch burn to a crisp right now. I'm convinced now more than ever that she's the devil and she is now threatening to bring me down.*

Instead of going home, I made a beeline to my uncle Eddie's apartment. I could've called him and had a conversation with him over the phone, but I knew that it wouldn't be wise to do that, especially with everything going on. So I hopped on the highway and headed in his direction.

I arrived at my uncle's apartment about fifteen minutes

after I left the Taco Bell. I parked my car between an old-ass pickup truck and my uncle Eddie's car. A pack of bad-ass kids almost ran over me while I climbed two flights of stairs. They had no supervision at all. I guess this was the new era of young mothers.

I knocked on the front door to my uncle's apartment and was greeted by Maggie. She smiled and welcomed me into the house. But before she closed the door, she peered around both corners. "Is my uncle here?" I asked her after she closed the front door and locked it. Before she could answer my question, he walked down the hallway towards me. He looked worried. More worried than he was before.

"What's going on? Is everything all right?" he wanted to know.

"Is there somewhere we can talk?" I asked him, but at the same time being respectful of his girlfriend.

He looked at Maggie without saying a word. "I'll go to the bedroom, but watch the food. Make sure it doesn't burn," she instructed him.

"Okay, I will," he assured her.

When Maggie got halfway down the hall, my uncle insisted that I take a seat on the sofa. And when she closed the door to the bedroom, he went into talk mode. "What, you went out to a party?"

"No, I was invited to a dinner."

"So, what's up?"

"The lady, Frances, had me meet her tonight so I could show her all the footage and photos I took earlier today. So, after she got to the end of it, she heard the conversation you and I had about you killing that guy earlier and how you gotta lay low for a while because of it."

"No way. How the hell did that thing record us talking?"

"I guess we made the mistake of pressing the wrong button. But whatever we did, it happened, and she heard it."

"What did she say?"

"Well, first of all, she didn't like the photos or the video footage I caught on the camera. She basically stated that it was garbage and she also said that if I don't find the incriminating evidence she can use by Friday, then she's gonna call the police and tell them who killed that guy and tell them that I know about it."

After hearing everything that I had just dropped into his lap, his facial expression turned from worry to rage. I've been knowing my uncle all my life and I know when he's about to erupt, and this was one of those times. "Yo, I swear to God, I would snap that bitch's throat if she opens her fucking mouth about me."

"Don't worry about her. I will take care of her."

"Did you see cops parked outside when you drove in the parking lot?"

"Nah, why?"

"Two homicide DTs knocked on the door last night and asked Maggie if I was here."

"Are you kidding me?" I asked him, even though I knew he wasn't lying to me. I just wanted clarity.

"Nope."

"So, what did Maggie tell them?"

"She told 'em that I didn't live here."

"Think they believed it?"

"At this point, they didn't have a choice. One of them did leave their business card."

"That means that they didn't believe her," I said. "I wonder how they knew to come here?"

"I think that little nigga that got away ratted me out."

"Oh no . . . that's not good," I said. "You do know that they will come back."

"Yeah, I know."

"So, what are you gonna do?"

"I'ma stay inside for a day or two. Hopefully, by then they'll set their sights somewhere else."

"Damn, this whole thing is insane. And to know that it had something to do with me, makes me feel so responsible."

"I don't know why, because I would've stepped to homeboy if it were Maggie. You know I don't take disrespect lightly."

I let out a long sigh because my uncle wasn't listening to me. Regardless of whoever he was taking up for, he took it too far. Now he was in this jam and no one would be able to get him out of it. Our town was small, so he was gonna get caught sooner than later.

I stayed over at my uncle's apartment for roughly about an hour, trying to figure out how he's going to deal with this ordeal. It seemed like every piece of advice I gave him, he shot it down. I figured at this point, he was gonna do what he wanted to do. The only thing about it, was that when he went back to prison, it would be because of me.

To clear my head, I didn't go straight home. Instead, I started driving around town trying to figure out what I could do in the next two days to get evidence that Frances's late husband didn't commit suicide and that he was murdered by one of his colleagues. Getting those pieces to the puzzle would be either hard or impossible.

Driving at night was something that I loved to do. I'd run down all of my windows and the sunroof. Turn on some oldies but goodies and just ride down whatever highway was near me. This was serenity for me. A way for me to put my worries on the back burner and just enjoy life for this very moment.

Twenty minutes into my drive, I started thinking of ways to get what Frances needed, even after she threatened to take me down with my uncle. Now I figured that the only way I could get closer to the cops was by having top-of-the-line bugging devices. I could put them in the car with ease. My uncle Eddie knew how to break into any car on these streets. The good part about it was that I wouldn't need him to do it physically. All I needed were instructions.

Armed with this idea, I turned my car and headed in the direction of Frances's home. I was going to call her and let her know that I was en route to her home, but then I decided against it. Knowing that she was on the detectives' radar, it wouldn't surprise me if they were monitoring her calls. So I put the pedal to the metal and drove over there.

Frances's neighborhood was quiet. Right before you enter the neighborhood, there's a sign posted at the corner letting everyone know that this neighborhood was being watched. Kudos to all the neighbors.

I drove a half mile farther into the neighborhood and found myself parked across the street from her house. But I aligned my car beside a truck to shield me from being detected if someone looked my way. Immediately after I powered off the ignition, I left my purse and the camera on the passenger seat and got out of the car. Excited about how I'd found a way to get Frances what she wanted, I strolled up the walkway. I saw two silhouettes walk by the living room mirror. I knew one of them looked like Frances's frame and the other one was a man. Puzzled by who it could be, I stood there, but as the door opened, I heard the voice and I shot behind a rose bush in her front yard. "You just take care of yourself and that little baby bump," I heard Detective Ryan Lopez say.

"Wait, what the fuck did he just say?" I mumbled to myself.

"I will. And I love you," I heard Frances say, and then I saw them kiss. It was a sensual one too. It wouldn't surprise me if they had just finished having sex because of the type of satin robe she was wearing. Not to mention how her hair was brushed up in a top knot.

"Call me when you get home, so I know that you got there safe."

"I will," he assured her, and then he hopped in his SUV.

Frances watched Ryan leave before she closed the front door, so I had to kneel down for what seemed like forever.

I thanked God after Ryan left. And when I rose up from behind the bush, I hauled ass back down the sidewalk and jumped back in my car. It took me less than a minute and a half to drive away from Frances's house. But I was also cautious not to run into Ryan during my ride to the nearest highway.

For the life of me, I couldn't wrap my head around what I just saw. Why was it that Frances hired me to find out who killed her late husband, but she was fucking one of his old colleagues? And to add fuel to the fire, she was not even pregnant by her late husband, she was pregnant by her side dude.

Ugh! How in the hell did I get in this jam? I am so fucking confused right now. One side of me wants to turn my car around and go and confront her. Let her know that I'm on to her. But then what's gonna happen next? She tells Ryan that I know about their secret and then he tries to kill me. Or blows my whole cover and acts like she didn't hire me to investigate those guys. If that happens, I'm screwed. The cops will go on a serious manhunt for me. What little information I have now will kill their careers on the force. Their pensions too. I've heard some stories about cops getting rid of whistle-blowers. Besides, who's gonna believe me over a cop? I can't think of anyone. Cops have a brotherhood and they take their shit to the grave.

Not able to talk to Frances about getting a listening device, and unable to go back to Uncle Eddie's house, I went home. After I walked in my apartment, I went straight to my bedroom and dropped everything on my bed. Then I got undressed and hopped in the shower. The water wasn't as hot as I would've liked it, but it served the purpose.

I climbed in my bed not too long after I got out of the shower, and my bed never felt so good. With what happened tonight still fresh on my mind, I tried to watch a movie on TV to block it out of my head, but it just wouldn't go anywhere. Knowing that Frances was playing mind games wasn't sitting well with me. She told me to spy on the very man she's sleeping with, and his boys.

17

MIDLIFE CRISES—UNCLE ED

Jamie hung out at the spot all last night, so when he came back to the house this morning, I was front and center. "What's up?" I greeted Jamie from the sofa. Maggie had left the apartment to go to the grocery store, which meant I had Jamie all to myself. I could talk to him like I do when we're at the spot, with no interruptions from Maggie.

"Nothing much," he replied as he closed the front door.

"Still can't find him, huh?" I asked him.

"Nah, and we beat the streets all last night," he replied as he headed into the kitchen. "Where's my mom?" he asked while he grabbed a bowl from a nearby cabinet, a box of cereal from the pantry, and the milk from the refrigerator.

"She went to the grocery store," I told him. But I was more concerned about that dude Bullet than where Maggie was.

After Jamie filled his bowl with the cereal and milk, he walked back to the living room and took a seat on the other sofa.

"Did you see any cops hanging outside? Or undercover cars parked anywhere near our building?" I asked.

"Nah, I didn't see 'em. And I was looking too," he said, and then he filled his mouth with a spoonful of cereal.

"Yeah, that's what they want us to think. But trust me, they're out there somewhere, waiting for me to walk out of this house so they can run up on me."

"Yeah, they might be," Jamie said between chews.

"I just wish that we could find that dude. He's fucking up my freedom. I don't wanna sit in this motherfucking house all day and every day. I wanna get out there and breathe some of that good air out there. But this bitch-ass nigga is fucking shit up for me," I expressed. The tension I was feeling on the inside was messing with my head.

"Don't worry, Ed, we are gonna find him. I put the word out to everybody I deal with on the streets, so as soon as they see him, they already got permission to snatch him up and take him to one of our spots."

"What kind of money you put on his head?"

"A grand."

"Nah, put another grand on it. I think two thousand dollars will make them dudes out there know that we're serious about getting this nigga off the streets."

"A'ight, you know I'm on it," he assured me, and then he changed his tone. "Yo, I'm sorry how shit went down between you and me yesterday. And I wanna say that I'm sorry for talking shit about Khloé. You're right, she is my family and I need to treat her that way."

"You know what, Jamie, I really appreciate you saying that. That was some grown-ass-man shit you just showed me. And I know it took a lot for you to say that too. So, I've got a newfound respect for you."

"Thanks, Ed. I appreciate you saying that."

"No problem. That's what I'm here for," I said. "Besides that, when you and me are getting along, it puts a smile on your mama's face."

"I know."

"Anything happen while you were out there last night?" I changed the subject. He and I knew how our relationship affected his mother, so there was no need to keep talking about it.

"The corner store on Lexington got raided. Somebody dropped dime and told the narc that those Indian dudes was selling bricks out of there."

"Damn! I knew they were selling weight out of there," I said with much disappointment.

"Well, the narcs got their shit now," Jamie replied, and then he got up from the chair. He walked in the kitchen, placed the bowl and the spoon in the sink and then he came back in the living room and sat back down. But as soon as he sat down, someone knocked on the front door. Anxiety struck me right in the middle of my chest and I jumped up from the sofa, but then I froze. "Want me to answer it?" Jamie asked me.

"I don't know. Think it could be somebody for you?" I whispered.

"Nah, Tony and Snoop dropped me off. And they know I ain't coming back out until later tonight."

Before I could utter another word, the person on the other side of the front door knocked three more times. "Think it might be the cops again?" Jamie asked me.

"I don't know. But I'm going in the bedroom," I told him, and then I raced down the hallway and disappeared into the room. After I closed the bedroom door and locked it, that's when I heard Jamie ask the person knocking to reveal themselves. "Who is it?"

"It's Mrs. Harris. Your probation officer," I heard a woman's voice say, and then I heard the front door open.

"I didn't know that you was coming here," I heard Jamie say.

"That's the point. Now are you going to let me in?"

"Oh yeah, my bad," Jamie commented. I could tell that he was nervous, and she could tell too.

"Is your mother here?"

"No."

"Is there anyone else in this apartment with you?"

Jamie hesitated and then he said, "No."

"Are you sure? Because I'm getting another vibe from you."

"Oh yeah, I'm sure."

"Have you found a job yet?"

"No. But I've been putting in a lot of applications online."

"Have you been smoking weed or using drugs?"

"Nope. I have a clean bill of health," Jamie replied with confidence. But I knew that he was lying. He smokes four to five blunts a day.

"So, if I test you right now, you'll pass it?"

"Yep," he assured her.

"Have you been hanging around any convicted felons?"

"Nope."

"Do you know if there are any convicted felons that live in this building?"

"I don't think so."

"Well, it'll be in your best interest to find out. Because if I come back here and see you talking or hanging out with someone that looks seedy, I'm gonna run their name through the system and if I find out that they're a felon, I will send you to jail."

"So, what am I supposed to do? Ask everybody that I come in contract with if they're a convicted felon?"

"Either do that or risk going to jail."

"Now, Mrs. Harris, you know that that's crazy. Whoever made that a rule was a straight-up hater."

"If you would stay out of trouble and do what you are supposed to do, then we wouldn't be having this conversation," she replied sarcastically. "Now let's take a walk through this apartment so that I can make sure that no one else is here."

"Wait, you gon' make sure no one is in this apartment?" he asked. He wanted to make sure he heard her correctly. If he didn't hear, I sure did. My heart fell into the pit of my stomach. And the thoughts in my head started going in a circular motion.

"Who did you say lives here again?" She repeated her question and it sounded like she had moved closer to me and Maggie's bedroom.

"Just me and my mom," he answered. He sounded like he was moving closer too.

"Well, that's not what I heard," she implied, and then I heard a door open.

"Why are you looking in the closet? There's nothing in there but shoes, coats, and boxes of my mom's old clothes."

I heard the door close and then I heard another door open. "Whatcha think, I'm hiding somebody in the bathroom?" Jamie's questions continued.

"Perhaps," she continued, and then I heard that door close. "This is your bedroom, right?" she asked him.

"Yep," Jamie replied. I heard them both walk into his bedroom. Seconds later, I heard his closet door open and then it closed.

"This must be your mother's bedroom, right?" she stated, and grabbed ahold of the doorknob. She wiggled the knob so she could come in me and Maggie's bedroom, but the lock stopped her.

"Yeah."

"Why is the door locked? Are you hiding something or someone in there?" Mrs. Harris pressed him.

"It's locked because it's my personal space and I don't want anyone going in there, especially when I'm not home,"

I heard Maggie say. I swear, I was never so happy to hear Maggie's voice coming from the other side of the door.

"Okay, I can understand that. But now that you're here, would you mind if I take a look in there?"

"Yes, I do mind. Now, if you don't remove yourself from my home, things could get really ugly," I heard Maggie threaten Jamie's probation officer.

"You do know that I can inspect his environment when I make home visits?" the probation officer informed Maggie.

"Not my house, you can't. Now when he gets his own place, you can walk into every room there, you can even spend the night too. But not here," Maggie continued. I swear, hearing my woman give that PO chick her ass to kiss made me feel liberated.

"Jamie, you may want to get a place of your own because as your PO, I should be able to walk anywhere I want."

"Well, when he gets a job, I will make sure he gets his own place. But until then, you're gonna have to abide by my rules."

"Jamie, sign this inspection form," Mrs. Harris instructed him as I heard her rattle a piece of paper. The room went silent for a couple of seconds. "Sign this one too," I heard her say and then another piece of paper rattled. "Okay, here is your copy. Call me in a few days so we can set up an office visit."

"Okay," Jamie told her and I heard the front door open and then it closed.

I waited for a moment to listen and see if the coast was clear. I didn't want to walk out of this bedroom and discover that for some reason Jamie's probation officer was still in the house.

"Is Eddie in the bedroom?" Maggie asked Jamie. And when she said that I knew that it was safe for me to come out of the bedroom.

By the time I unlocked the bedroom door and opened it,

Maggie was standing front and center. She smiled and said, "I know you're getting tired of hiding in our room every time someone comes to our front door."

I took a deep breath and then I exhaled. "Pretty much," I answered as we turned around and headed down the hallway. I followed her into the kitchen.

"That was a close call, huh?" Jamie mentioned.

"You damn right it was," I agreed. "If your mama hadn't come in the house, and I hadn't locked the bedroom door, that lady would've walked in there."

"I'm glad I came in here when I did," Maggie added.

"Me too," I replied.

"What did she say when she walked in the house?" Maggie wanted to know.

"She ran through a list of questions about me not being able to hang out with convicted felons, if she gave me a piss test would I pass it, and then she asked me if there was somebody lived here other than you. I told her no on every question."

"Yeah, he said no, but she still walked her nosey ass around here and started looking for shit that didn't concern her."

"Ed ain't lying, Ma. She looked around the living room, she peeped her head in the kitchen, she looked in closets, and she even looked in the bathroom. When she saw that the bathroom shower had a glass door, she closed the door. After she didn't see anything out of place in my room, she wanted to look in yours next."

"Sounds like she was looking for you," Maggie told me.

"I was thinking the same thing, because all the police got to do is run a home address and whoever lives there, their criminal record will pop up. And when that happens, they can find out if two convicted felons have the same address on file," I agreed.

"Which is why the cops probably called your PO and told

her to come and check out your residence. They figured since they don't have a search warrant to search this house, your PO can," Maggie added.

"Y'all might be right, because she's been over here a lot of times, and she never looked through here like that before," Jamie realized. He was finally seeing the light.

Maggie chimed back in. "Well, thank God that I came in this house when I did. Because I can't be trying to bail my son and my man out of jail at the same time."

"Believe me, I ain't trying to go to jail," Jamie insisted.

"Me either," I stated. At this point, the only person standing in the way of me going to jail was that dude Bullet. *He needs to be found and I mean now.*

18

WICKED WAYS—KHLOÉ

With the night that I had last night, I chose to sleep late this morning. I mean, what better time to regroup from all the shit I went through last night? Not only did I run into a disgusting-ass cop, I found out that Frances has been playing games behind my back. *If I'm dreaming, please wake me up.*

I realized that it was close to noon when my cell phone rang. After I grabbed it, I also realized that the call was coming from Farrah Gomez. Ugh! I knew she was gonna wanna talk me to death about why I left her party last night. She might even give me attitude too. Well, I guess that I would see.

"Hello," I said, trying to sound groggy. I figured if she thought that she woke me up, then she'd keep this conversation short and sweet.

"I'm sorry, were you asleep?" she asked me.

"What time is it?" I hit her with a question.

"It's almost twelve o'clock. I thought that you'd be up by now," she reasoned.

"It's okay," I lied. And I was laughing on the inside because my plan was working.

"Well, look, I only called to find out what happened to you last night. When I turned around you were gone. Was everything all right?"

"Oh, Farrah, I'm sorry. When I went back to the bathroom, I started feeling sick, so I went home. I should've told you that I was leaving. My bad."

"Oh no, it's okay. I just wanted to make sure that everything was all right with you," she said. "So, did you have a nice time while you were here?" Her questions continued.

"I had a ball. So thank you for inviting me. Oh, and that cop guy named Brad was funny. His wife was really nice too," I mentioned. I needed to set a trap and see if she showed her hand.

"Yes, Brad and Kate are a great couple. They complement each other so well."

"Yes, they do."

So let me ask you," I said, changing the direction of the conversation. "Are you going to that Norfolk city detective honoring ceremony the day after tomorrow? I'm sure if your husband is going, I know you're gonna be there."

"What honoring ceremony? There's no honoring ceremony the day after tomorrow."

"Wait, so Norfolk isn't honoring the narcotics and homicide detectives the day after tomorrow?" I pressed the issue.

"Not to my knowledge, and I would know because I work at headquarters. Maybe you got the cities and districts wrong."

"Yeah, I must have. So, let's get together sometime next week. I would love to hang out and do lunch with you," I said, even though I couldn't care less if I saw her again. My mission to get close to her and milk her for information was accomplished. Now I could move on to my next mission.

"Oh, I would love that. Maybe then we can catch up and talk about old times." Farrah seemed excited by the idea.

"Yes, that would be really fun. So call me," I told her.

"I will," she assured me, and then our call went radio silent.

With my cell phone in hand, I stood up from my bed and started pacing. The thought of that bitch Frances lying to me about Brad and his boys attending a ceremony in the next couple of days infuriated me. Why lie? Why say that she needed to get her late husband's colleagues arrested before the ceremony? I mean, what was going on in her head? And what was I supposed to do now?

"I'm gonna get this bitch on the phone now," I said to myself as my blood started boiling through my veins. "Calm down, Khloé. You gotta keep your composure, girl. You can't let that bimbo see your hand. Stay ahead of her until you can peep at her cards," I mumbled underneath my breath. And it was true, I couldn't let her know what I just found out. I had to play her game, and that's what I intended to do.

I dialed her number and it started ringing instantly. She answered my call on the fourth ring. "Hey, Frances, how are you?" I started the dialog.

"Hi, Khloé, I'm doing good. Thanks for asking. And you're gonna live long because I was just thinking about calling you," she said.

"Great minds think alike, huh?"

She chuckled. "You can say that again. So, what's up? Got any good news for me?"

"I was wondering, would you be inclined to get me some wiretaps for all the cops' cars? This would definitely help with the timing of everything, since you want me to solve your husband's murder within the next couple of days."

"No, putting wiretaps on all of their cars would be too

risky. And knowing how paranoid they all are, they'll find it faster than the time it took us to install it."

"You really think so?" I asked her. I wanted to appear like I was doing my due diligence to help her crack this bogus-ass case she conjured up in her sick head.

"Just do what I say. I'm the boss, okay?" she snapped. I hadn't ever heard her talk to me like this before. So, I brought it to her attention.

"Are you all right? Are your hormones off track a little?" I asked her.

"Yes, I'm just fine. Why do you ask?"

"Because you've never talked to me like that before. I thought that maybe you were having a bad day. Or something."

She fell silent and then she said, "Yes, I guess you can say that I'm being hormonal right now. Pregnancy makes you have all different kinds of mood swings," she said. Now it sounded like she was going into overkill. But I knew the real reason. I was getting underneath her skin and she wasn't happy about it.

"Oh, it's all right. Sorry that I got you upset," I managed to say while clenching my jaw.

"Oh, don't worry about it. So, what's on today's agenda? Going back out to do more surveillance work?"

"Yep, I'm gonna leave out of here within the hour."

"Perfect. Well, if you need anything or just need to talk, don't hesitate to call me. And don't forget, the honoring ceremony is right around the corner," she reminded me. I swear, I wanted to blast her ass and tell her I knew that there was no fucking ceremony. But I played it cool. She had some shit brewing, and if I just pick and choose my battles with her, I'd find out what was really going on and win the war.

"Are you attending that ceremony?" I asked and waited for her answer.

"I thought about it. But no, I wouldn't give those bastards the time of day."

"Think I could go?"

"Why would you want to go? There's nothing spectacular that's gonna happen. Remember I hired you to investigate those crooked-ass motherfuckers. The plan is to get them arrested so that they can't attend the ceremony themselves. Now let me get off the phone so you can go out and handle our business. Don't forget to call me if you need something."

"Will do," I said, and then I disconnected our call.

Immediately after I pressed the red button on my cell phone, I shook my head with disgust. That lying-ass bitch just gave me one lie after the other. And I still didn't know what her motives were. But I would find out sooner than later.

It took me less than thirty minutes to get dressed. I grabbed my car keys and my purse and headed out the front door. I went to the same electronics boutique where Frances bought the video camera equipment. I was greeted by an older white gentleman as soon as I walked in the small store. He looked like Santa Claus without the costume. "How can I help you, young lady?" he didn't hesitate to say.

"Hi, sir, I'm looking for some wiretap devices. Something small and inexpensive."

"When you say inexpensive, what budget are you working with? And where do you want to put these wiretaps?"

"See, it's like this. I have a boyfriend and he and my best friend are very close. I don't trust either one of them, so I would like to put listening devices in each of their cars," I explained. I thought I sounded sincere. And hopefully he could help me out.

"Sounds like you are in a pickle." He smiled.

"I won't be for long."

"Okay, so I have two wiring devices in mind." He reached underneath a glass display counter and pulled out two small cases that were probably the same size as a box of cigarettes. "Here's my best-selling product in the store. This is the Enduro Black Box Recorder. This is the ideal audio recorder for a number of reasons. Firstly, it's discreet. The device is very nondescript and the fact it is pocket-sized makes it perfect for those recording audio while on the go and ideal for long-term deployment, especially within a car or other vehicle. It has voice activation capabilities, which means that when no one is talking, this device conserves battery life extremely well. As a matter of fact, this listening device can remain in standby mode for 166 days. This recorder is also highly versatile as it is compatible with both Windows and Mac computers and the sensitivity of the microphone gives it a ten-meter radius."

"Wow! How much does this device coast?"

"It'll run you around four hundred dollars. And believe me, it's worth every penny."

"Don't worry. I believe you. But show me the other wiring device," I insisted.

"Okay, here's the Hawk Spyware parabolic microphone," he said, and showed me a small satellite-dish shaped receiver. "This listening device is designed for long-distance listening. It can be aimed in any direction to pick up conversations from hundreds of feet away."

"I like this one better. How much is it?"

"This one is a little over eight hundred dollars. But I was okay with it because, you don't have to plant the device in someone's car. All you have to do is point in the direction you want to go."

"Okay, that's a no-brainer. I'm gonna go with the Hawk Spy device," I told him.

"Perfect. And what method of payment are you using today?" he asked.

"Visa," I said, and handed him my credit card.

"Great. I'll be right back," he said, and walked away from the counter. Moments later, he had my device boxed and bagged up with the credit card receipt in hand.

"I can't believe that it was this fast to get what I needed," I pointed out while I signed the credit card receipt.

"I aim to please." The salesman smiled.

"Thank you," I said, and then I walked out of the store, holding my purchase in hand.

I couldn't get home fast enough to check out my new spy device. I was geeked up like a kid in a candy store. That whole conversation I had earlier with Frances's lying ass kind of evaporated into thin air. She just didn't know that I was about to see her for who she truly was. On the surface I could tell that she tried to act like the victim, but I knew she was a snake, and I was gonna prove it too.

After I unboxed everything, I read the instructions one by one. Initially I was intimidated, but when I walked myself slowly through each step, it got easier.

I wanted to check out my merchandise and see how great it was. I thought about leaving my apartment to search for an easy candidate; but when I looked outside and saw one of my female neighbors visibly upset while she was on her cell phone and sitting in her car, I turned on my device and aimed the disk in her direction. Her conversation lit up my microphone. It also helped that she had her call on speaker. "Why are you doing this to me? You know that I love you," she cried. Her name was Leslie. I didn't know her on a personal level. But I did know that she was a young college student and she lived with two more roommates who were probably around her same age. They lived five doors down from me. From what I could see, she was a cute girl. But according to this phone call, she was dealing with a load of self-esteem issues. "Leslie, I just need some time to myself. That's it," I heard the guy say.

"Is it somebody else?"

"No, it's not."

"Then what is it?"

"Look, Leslie, you know my mom is having a hard time right now because of my dad passing, and she needs me."

"You're acting like you don't have other brothers and sisters. They can pitch in and be with your mother most of the time."

"Leslie, let's just drop it. Nothing you say is going to change my mind."

"Why don't you just keep it real? You know I know that your ex-girlfriend is close with your mother, and she's gonna be spending a lot of time there and that's why you want this break between us."

The guy let out a long sigh. "It doesn't matter what I say, you're gonna think the way you want."

"That's because I know what you're saying is bullshit."

"Look, I'm done with this," he said, and then he ended the call. This infuriated her. Within seconds, she started calling him back. But her call went straight to voicemail. She called once more, and yet again, the call went directly to voicemail. "He thinks he's gonna hang up on me and then block me. Not today," she said, and then she sped off.

After Leslie drove away, I knew I had the real-deal listening device in my hands. It was so easy and simple. And I was ready to go on the road with it. I called Uncle Eddie since I hadn't heard from him today. "Hey, Unc, what's up?" I started off saying.

"The same shit. Different day."

"Have you been out of the apartment yet?"

"I wish, 'cause this shit is driving me crazy."

"How is Maggie?"

"She's cool with it because she likes when I'm in the house. She can keep tabs on me that way."

"Is she there?"

"Yeah, she's in the shower."

"I've got some shit to tell you, but I know I can't get into it now. But if it's all right, I'd like to stop by and see you later."

"Yeah, but make sure it's dark outside."

"I gotcha, don't worry," I assured him. "Well, let me get off this phone. Got a lot of shit I need to take care of."

"A'ight. Be careful and I'll see you later."

"Perfect."

I wanted to try my satellite Hawk Spy device on Detective Brad and his flunkies, but I decided against it because it was too early in the day. I figured when they went on shift tonight, my time would be more productive because I would have all four of them together. But I set my sights on Frances. She was probably home conjuring up evil plots against everybody and everyone. But not for long, because once I figured out what her angle was, I would shut her lying ass down.

When I pulled up on the street that Frances lived on, I decreased my speed so I wouldn't bring any attention to myself because I am considered a local celebrity news reporter. I also did it just in case her side boy-toy Ryan's car was parked near her place. Didn't want him sitting in the car doing something else and end up seeing me riding by. I can't have her seeing me riding by her place either, especially unannounced. If that happened, it would send up red flags immediately.

Thankfully, the coast was clear. None of her neighbors were out. I didn't see any landscaping workers walking around. Nor was her side man Ryan's car parked in the general area of her house. Her car was parked out there, though.

I found a parking space on the opposite side of a white commercial van. It looked like it belonged to someone that lived on this block. After I powered off my car, I positioned myself and aimed the disk directly at Frances's house, but I couldn't pick up her voice. All I heard was dead air. So I powered off the device and then I turned it back on. But still I heard nothing. "Why isn't this working?" I asked myself, my words barely audible. I powered off the device again and turned it back on for the third time. Frustrated, I placed the device on my lap, grabbed my cell phone from the cup holder near my gearshift, and dialed Frances's cell phone number. "Hey, Frances, do you have a minute?" I asked her and then I pressed the mute button.

"Sure. Is everything all right?" she wanted to know. And at that moment, I heard Frances's voice, but it wasn't that clear, so I lifted the satellite device and pointed towards Frances's house and that's when her voice became clear. Now, I knew that I couldn't talk to her and work the device at the same time, so I turned it off.

"I think I'm on to something," I started off saying. I needed to say something to her that would get her riled up. Maybe add Ryan to the equation and see if her mood changed. Who knows, if I got her upset enough, she might get Ryan to come to her house or call him on the phone. However she did it, it needed to get done.

"What do you mean?"

"Now I know you said that you know that your late husband didn't commit suicide. And you strongly believe that he was murdered by one of his cop friends. With that said, do you think that the cop Ryan could've done it? He is the rookie of the bunch, which means that you gotta prove yourself. Show the older guys that you're worthy to be in their circle."

"No, I don't think he's the one that killed Gavin. I think Brad and Chris Lemon did it. So that's where you need to focus your attention."

"Why don't you think that Ryan could be involved?" I pressed her.

"Because I have the gut feeling that Brad and Chris did it."

"But what if I found out that Ryan did have something to do with it?"

"Look, Khloé, Ryan and Gavin were cool with each other. On the other hand, Brad and Chris started beefing with Gavin around two weeks before Gavin was found dead. Not only that, I heard Brad threaten Gavin many times, so just take my word for it. Time is winding down and I don't need you wasting your time on an issue I know too well."

"Okay, no problem. I'll take your word for it," I replied apologetically. But I was jumping for joy on the other end of my phone. She was taking my bait and it was only a matter of time when I would be able to pull off all the layers covering her butt.

"Great. Now is there something else you wanted to share with me?"

"No, that's all I wanted."

"So, who are you going after today?" Her tone changed.

"I'm gonna follow your lead and go after Brad and Chris. Hopefully, by the end of the night I'll have some really good information for you."

"Perfect! Okay, so, I'll wait to hear from you. Now be careful out there. And remember after today, we only have two more days."

"I'm on it," I assured her. Immediately after I ended our call, I grabbed the satellite disk, powered it on, and then I pointed it directly at Frances's house. Within several seconds, her voice came through the listening device with ease.

"Who the hell does she think she is?" I heard her say, as she shuffled things around. I couldn't figure out what they were, but I could say that I made her extremely angry. A few seconds later I heard a cell phone ringing, so I knew that she was making a call. I also knew that she placed her call on speaker, which was a bonus for me.

"Hello," I heard a man's voice say.

"You will not fucking believe it," she spat.

"What happened?" the guy asked.

"I just got off a call with Khloé, and she comes up with this bright idea about how she thinks that you killed Gavin."

And that's when I knew she was talking to Ryan.

"*What?*" he replied. "What made her come up with that assumption?"

"She was like, hey, Frances, I believe that cop Ryan was the one that killed Gavin. And I was like, what makes you say that, and then she says that by you being the rookie of the bunch, you're gonna have to prove yourself worthy of being in their group, especially 'cause of all the narcotics police officers' reputations."

"What, she thinks we're in the movie *Training Day?*" he said, and then he chuckled.

"Ryan, why are you laughing? This is not fun and games. You know this girl is good at what she does. So we've gotta keep her focused on Brad, Chris, and Nick."

"Stop stressing. Everything is going to be all right."

Frances let out a long sigh. "I just wish that things were different. If Gavin hadn't found out about the baby, he'd still be alive. And we could've all gotten our piece of the pie and gone our separate ways," Frances declared. And for the first time, she sounded apologetic.

"If Gavin would've stuck to the original plan, he wouldn't be dead. You saw how much Internal Affairs was breathing down his neck. Remember, he threatened to tell them everything we had going on, so he put that shit on himself."

"I know, I know. It's just that every time I go into his closet and see his stuff packed away, I start feeling guilty."

"I told you to take his shit out of there!" Ryan snapped.

This was the first time in their phone call that I heard him get loud. I had clearly gotten to them.

"I will," she said, trying to pacify him.

"But you keep saying it."

"Well, if I'm taking so long to do it, then why don't you come over here and do it yourself?"

"That's all I needed to hear," he replied sarcastically.

"And what does that mean?"

"It means, just how I said it," he said with annoyance. "Look, let's drop it because we're going in circles. Right now, we need to put our focus on getting Brad, Chris, and Nick out of the way, cover our tracks, and get this money. From there, it'll be me, you, and our little baby boy on a beach in California, living life."

"You make it sound so easy, like you can snap your fingers and *poof*, we're there."

Before Ryan elaborated more on his future plans with Frances and their baby, he interjected, "Hey, baby, let me go. Brad just texted me to call him."

"Think it's about our cargo?"

"Yeah, I do. So I'll call you back later."

"What time to you go in tonight?" she asked him.

"My shift starts at eight, but I'll probably call you back before then."

"Okay. I love you," she told him.

"I love you too," he said, and then their call went radio silent.

Instantly filled up with a ton of emotions tossing and turning in my stomach almost made me have a panic attack. The thoughts in my head started scrambling out of control. When I planned to eavesdrop in on Frances's cell phone calls, I never thought in my wildest dreams that I would stumble on this type of information. This was a lot of shit to take on, especially the part about Frances knowing exactly what happened to her late husband. And how much money was Frances and Ryan talking about? Whatever amount it was, Ryan and Frances didn't want to split it with Brad, Chris, or Nick.

Right before Ryan ended the call, he mentioned that Brad had texted him. And right off the bat, Frances wanted to know if it was about the *cargo*. My only question now was, what kind of cargo was she talking about? Was this cargo what Internal Affairs had wanted to talk to Gavin about?

19

STREET LIFE—UNCLE ED

All day long, I watched the streets from the living room window. I was bored as fuck. It's one thing to hang out in the house all day because you choose to. But when you can't go out because the cops are looking for you, it's tough. It's a feeling like they have control of me. Like I'm in jail under twenty-three-hour lockdown. Thankfully, I've got my woman with me to cook and give some of her loving. If I didn't, I'd be one upset motherfucker!

Since Jamie had done an overnighter in the streets, he chilled in the house for a few hours to rest up. When he got up around four o'clock, I sent him back in the streets and encouraged him to have a huge manhunt so that he and his boys could find Bullet. "Whatcha want me to do with him if we find him?" Jamie wanted to know.

"FaceTime, because I wanna watch you and those other niggas torture the hell outta his ass," I instructed him.

"You got it," he said, and then he hit the streets.

The sun went down around seven thirty, and Khloé stopped by as she promised. And boy, was I happy to see her.

"See any cops out there?" I asked her after Maggie let her in the apartment.

"No, I didn't. And I was looking too," she told me while giving me a hug. I took a seat on the sofa and she sat in the love seat.

"Want something to drink, Khloé?" Maggie asked.

"I just had a smoothie on the way here. Thanks anyway."

"You're welcome. What about you, babe? Want me to get you something before I go in the bedroom?" Maggie asked me while standing in the middle of the living room floor.

"No, I'm good. Thank you, though."

"All right. Well, if y'all need anything, just holla," she said, and then she went into our bedroom.

"Uncle Ed, I've got so much shit to tell you," Khloé said, and then she paused, I guess trying to gather her thoughts.

I pushed her to talk. "What's up?"

"I went out and bought a listening device so that when I go out following those rat-ass niggas, I can hear their entire conversations," she started off saying.

"What kind did you get?"

"It's one of those satellite-disk-looking devices. All I have to do is point it in the direction I want to pick up voices, and then the sound comes through about a couple seconds later."

"So, have you used it yet?" I wanted to know.

"As a matter of fact, I did. I went to Frances's fucking house and sat outside in my car and heard her have an entire conversation with the narc cop Ryan. The Hispanic guy."

"Yeah, I know who he is."

"But you ain't gonna believe this shit. I don't know if I told you this, but she's pregnant. And her dead husband isn't the father. Ryan is the father. And guess what else?"

"What?"

"She didn't hire me to find out if her husband committed

suicide or not, she knows that he was killed. She knew he was going to get killed before he did."

"Who murked him?"

"I don't know that yet. But something happened and Internal Affairs started an investigation. Gavin threatened to blow the whistle on whatever they had going on, and they wasn't having it, so they killed him and made it look like a suicide."

"Wait, so you heard all that through that satellite thing?"

"Yes."

"So, what are you going to do now?"

"I haven't figured that out just yet, but I do know that I'm gonna still follow those bastards around. I may even use the shit I've gotten to blackmail her grimy ass. She and Ryan mentioned something about getting a big payoff in the next day or so, so I may be able to squeeze more money out of her ass. What do you think?"

"I think that's a good idea. But we've got to figure out how much it is, where it's at, and how we're gonna get it."

"I will, don't worry."

"So, are you going out tonight?"

"Yes, as soon as I leave here, I'm going to ride downtown and see if I can catch them with their pants down."

"I want you to be careful."

"Come on now, you know I can handle myself," she said, I guess trying to brush me off. "Oh yeah, I forgot to tell you that there's no freaking honoring ceremony for the cops. Frances lied. She gave me that time crunch because she had another agenda. And tonight, I hope I find out what it is."

While Khloé and I talked about those dirty-ass cops, my cell phone started ringing. "Hold on, Khloé, this is Jamie FaceTiming me," I told her.

"Oh, go ahead," she said as she scooted back on the sofa another inch or two.

"What's up, J?" I asked after he appeared on my Apple phone.

"Where is my mom?" he asked me. He seemed like he was kind of amped up and eager to talk.

"She's in the bedroom. Why? You want her?"

"Nah, I just didn't want her around when I tell you what I gotta tell you." He sounded a little winded.

"You good. Go ahead," I insisted.

While I waited for him to tell me exactly why he called me, he took his cell phone from his face and flipped the camera. And *boom* there he was, Bullet duct-taped to a chair with his mouth bound with gray electric tape. I swear, this made me a very happy man.

I became giddy. "No fucking way! You got that son of a bitch!"

"Who? That guy Bullet?" Khloé whispered to me. And then she stood up, walked over and took a seat next to me. She followed by leaning in towards me so she could see what it was that I was looking at. Seeing Bullet's bloody face, duct taped, she had a knee-jerk reaction and scooted away from me.

"Oh my God! Look at his face. You can't even see his eyes," she whispered, trying to grapple with what she just saw.

"Where did you find him?" I asked Jamie.

"He was chilling at the house of this girl we know out in Huntersville. As soon as I put out the word on the ransom, homegirl found out about it and gave him up," Jamie replied, and then he burst into laughter. "Somebody needs to tell him that bitches ain't loyal," Jamie continued.

"Turn the phone around so he can see my face," I instructed Jamie.

"There he go. He can see you now," Jamie insisted.

"Nigga, all I want you do to is nod your head when I ask you questions. *You dig?*" I roared at him like I was literally in his face. Without giving Khloé a moment's notice, I grabbed her by the arm and yanked her towards me. I even turned my cell phone around so this dude could see her face. Khloé sat there, helpless and confused it seemed like. Her facial expression was between shocked and horrified. "Do you see her?"

Bullet nodded his head.

"This is my niece. You talked major shit about her, and no one does that to a member of my family, which is why you're in the predicament now." I frowned at him while gritting my teeth together. "Now tell me, did you go to the cops?"

Bullet shook his head no.

"That's bullshit! The cops came looking for me, so I know you're lying. Now, I'm gonna ask you one more time, did you rat me out to the cops?" I roared. This time the veins in my face were bulging.

Bullet hesitated. So Jamie hit him with the butt of a gun across his head. "Answer him," Jamie snapped.

The pain from the blow to Bullet's skull forced him to scream out. His cry was muffled from the tape, but I could see the agony he was going through.

Khloé jerked away from me. It was evident that she didn't want to see it. But I wasn't having it. I was doing this for her. And she was going to see just how far I would go for her. So as delicately as I could, I pulled her back towards me. "No, no, no, you're gonna see this. I'm doing this for you," I told her, and then I turned my attention back to Bullet—and Jamie, who stood over top of him.

"Jamie, what did he say? Did he admit to ratting me out?"

"I don't know. After I hit him in the head he screamed like a little bitch!"

"Are you on the phone with Jamie?" Maggie asked. She popped out of nowhere. She stood at the entryway of the hallway and the living room. Khloé shot a look at Maggie like a deer in the headlights.

"Yeah, it's Jamie. He's doing something for me," I said calmly. I didn't want her to get upset about what was going on.

She pressed the issue. "What is he doing?"

"Can I use the bathroom?" Khloé asked Maggie, and stood up before Maggie could answer her.

"You know where it is," Maggie replied and moved out of the way so Khloé could walk by.

"Please don't do this right now. Let me handle this and I'll come and talk to you in a minute." I tried to reason with Maggie. She looked like she was about to resist because she hesitated. But then she said, "Come in the room as soon as Khloé leaves."

"I will, baby," I assured her, and watched her walk away.

I turned back towards Jamie standing next to Bullet. "Tell that dude he got one more chance to answer my question," I started off saying.

"He can hear you. He can see you too," Jamie announced.

"Bullet, did you rat me out to the cops?" I repeated the question.

He nodded his head. And when he nodded his head, acknowledging that he did give the cops my name, I instantly became numb. It felt like I was in a trance. But then I shook it off and became enraged. I wished that I was in front of that dude right now. I swear, I would've ripped his fucking throat out. When you become a member of our organization, snitching to the cops will get you killed immediately, and he knew this when he joined. Never mind the fact that I killed his cousin. Everyone knows the rules. Mothers, sisters, kids, grandmothers, uncles, and aunts are not exempt. Everyone that rats another member out will be killed on sight.

"Jamie, find out exactly what he told the cops and I'll see you later, a'ight."

"I gotcha!" he said and then we ended the call.

A few minutes later, Khloé came out of the bathroom. She looked stressed out. "You a'ight?" I asked her. But I knew she wasn't. I just wanted to see how her mind was after seeing what I showed her.

"No, but I will be," she replied as she made her way towards the front door.

"Hey, wait, I don't get a hug?" I smiled, trying to lighten up the mood. Unfortunately, it didn't work.

"Unc, you know I love you. But I gotta go," she said, and then she let out this forced smile. And when she forced herself to smile, I knew that she had had enough. I hoped sooner than later that she would see that I was doing this for her.

20

LEAVE ME ALONE—KHLOÉ

Iswear, I couldn't get out of my uncle's apartment quick enough. I know that I've covered murders and kidnappings and even seen dead bodies lying in pools of blood, when I was a field journalist; but to actually see someone being tortured in front of me was on another level. Besides that, I didn't want to witness someone being murdered. That goes against everything that I stand for. I'm not certain, but it seemed like Maggie was also against it. I mean, why would she come out of the bedroom to chastise my uncle like that and be okay with it? She was probably more upset because her son was involved.

I took a deep breath and exhaled after I turned on the ignition. I had to get in a renewed headspace so that I could drive home safely. Dealing with everything I had on my plate, all at the same time, was starting to weigh me down. I didn't know how much more I could take, but I did know that the time was nearing.

"Excuse me, can you kids get out of the way?" I yelled politely at the crowd of kids playing dodge ball.

Slowly, as they moved out of my way, I was able to drive farther out of the parking lot. As soon as I broke free of the little mob, I made a right turn to get onto the next street, only to be cut off and blinded by the headlights of a car driven by Norfolk's Finest. Instantly a wave of anxiety engulfed me and I couldn't do anything about it. My window was rolled up, so I rolled it down as two white cops in plain clothes approached me. "Act calm, Khloé, you got this, girl," I coached myself, my words barely audible.

"Can you tell me why you're blocking me from leaving?" I asked the cop that stepped up to my driver-side door. I looked over at the cop on the passenger side of my car as he posted up and watched me from his angle.

"Can I see your license, registration, and proof of insurance?"

"Not until you tell me why you're blocking me from leaving." I tested him. *I mean, who the hell does he think he is? I haven't done anything wrong.*

"You're in a high drug-trafficking area and we want to make sure that you haven't committed any crimes," he finally answered me.

"Do you know who I am?" I asked him. I was getting angrier by the second.

"If I did, then I wouldn't need to see your license, proof of insurance, and registration."

"Well, so that you know, I am Khloé Mercer, the news journalist, and I don't use drugs, so therefore I wouldn't need to buy drugs," I responded sarcastically.

"Oh yeah, I knew you looked familiar." He smiled.

"Well, if she's not a drug user, then tell us, why are you out here?" the other cop interjected.

"I was visiting a friend," I lied, and he knew it too. So what was I supposed to say, I just left from seeing my uncle?

"Who's your friend?"

"Her name is Trina."

"What's Trina's last name?" The cop on the other side pressed the issue.

"I don't know her last name."

"Bullshit!" the other cop replied. "We know your uncle Eddie Mercer lives with his girlfriend and her son in that apartment building."

"Well, if that's what you think, then so be it," I stated. I wasn't backing down from these fools. I knew my rights, and they knew I knew them too.

"Ms. Mercer, why don't you play fair with us and tell us where your uncle is. All we wanna do is ask him a few questions."

"Damn, it sounds like you guys know more than me. And I don't know what else to say."

"You do know that if you know where he is, we could charge you with interfering with a murder case?" the cop to my left said.

"Okay, now I know you guys are crazy," I said, and pressed the power button to roll my window back up. "Please move out of my way. And if you don't, I will call your supervisor," I yelled at them.

"So, you aren't gonna help us out? We could help your uncle out if you just tell us where he is," the cop to my left insisted.

"Move your fucking car now! If you don't, I will make a report to your supervisor right now," I threatened, and then I showed them my cell phone.

The cop to my left told his partner to back off, and then they both walked away from my car. After they got back in their car, the cop who was driving backed it up and then they veered out of my path so I could drive away. The second after I made a right turn onto the next street, my nerves began to calm down. My heart rate slowed down and so did my breathing. At one point, it felt like I was hyperventilating.

I couldn't think straight. I was just a big ball of mess. But thank God that with every mile I drove, I started regaining my sense of self.

Five minutes into my drive, I knew that I had to call my uncle and tell him what had just happened. I couldn't have him roaming around that apartment like a sitting duck. He needed to know what was going on outside his door. "Unc, I just wanted to let you know that the cops blocked me from leaving the parking lot of your building. They ended up letting me leave, but they know you're either in the house or that you live there, so please be careful."

"What did they say after they walked up on you?"

"They asked me for my driver's license, registration—you know, and the rest of the stuff. So I asked them why did they want to see my credentials? And they gave me some ol' bogus excuse about I was leaving a high drug-trafficking area and they just needed to see who I was. But check it out, they already knew who I was. And after I called them out on their bullshit, they started begging me to tell them where you were. Talking about all they wanna do is talk to you about the murder."

"And what did you say?"

"I told them that I didn't know where you were. So they were like, then who were you visiting? And I told them that I was visiting a friend of mine named Trina. But they didn't believe me."

"So, how did you get them to let you go?"

"Whatcha mean, let me go? I know my rights, and I let them know that too. So when I threatened to call their superior, they carried their asses."

Uncle Ed chuckled. "Now that's what I am talking about. Show those crackers that you don't take no shit from them!"

"You better watch your back, because they're out there and they're waiting on you to slip up," I warned him.

"Good looking-out, niece!" he replied with gratitude.

He and I said a few more words and then I ended the call, especially after he told me in so many words that that guy Bullet wasn't in the picture. It was obvious that my uncle was a product of the streets and I wanted no part of it.

At the last minute, I changed my mind about going home. I figured that if I did, I'd be losing time to meet Frances's deadline and I'd lose the momentum I had before I had gone to see my uncle. I was already on track to connect the dots between Frances and Ryan. Now all I had to do was add Brad, Chris, and Nick to the equation and I'd have done my job.

According to Ryan from his conversation with Frances earlier, his shift with the other guys started at eight p.m. It was nine thirty now, so I turned my car around and headed downtown to the roughest housing projects of Norfolk. Uncle Ed had already taken me on the routes that the narcs frequent, so that's where I went.

I drove to Young's Park first. I rode through the horseshoe and it was quiet. I saw a few small-time dealers out there, but nothing that would give me some traction. I drove to Kerry Park housing authority next. That's the project where that narc picked up that young girl and made her suck his dick. I knew for sure that those morons would be there. But unfortunately, they weren't. My third spot was Huntersville. Huntersville was a section in Norfolk where the sale of heroin ran rampant. Junkies swarmed that place, so there was no doubt in my mind that those scumbags were riding around to catch their next prey. Huntersville was designed with a bunch of one-way streets. It was a good thing and a bad thing all at one time. If you're looking for someone, they could be on the next street over and you wouldn't know it. The two-way streets had their advantages. You could ride by the person you were looking for and run right into them. The downside was that if you ran into someone that you'd been trying to avoid, then you were fucked. Simple as that.

So as I made my way down every street in Huntersville, my search came up empty. I was becoming extremely frustrated, and when I realized that my hunt for the cops was fruitless, I exited the neighborhood and headed to the next one. For the entire drive throughout Norfolk, I couldn't find those bastards anywhere. I even rode by their district office and they weren't there. I became so annoyed. Of all nights, I couldn't find these assholes. But then it dawned on me to call Frances. I knew if I got her on the phone and made an inquiry about Ryan and the rest of the guys, she'd get him on the phone. Hopefully, somewhere in their conversation she'd give me a clue as to where they were.

21

THE DOG HOUSE—UNCLE ED

Maggie has been on my ass all night about getting Jamie involved in my beef with that Bullet dude. It was a couple of hours since it happened, and she wouldn't stop talking about it. And when Jamie came in the house to clean himself up, the whole argument shit started back up.

She stood at the entryway of his bedroom while I stood alongside of her. Jamie wasn't feeling this whole argument thing, but he had no choice but to stay there and listen to her. *"What, you trying to go to jail?"* she roared.

"Ma, you know this comes with the territory. And besides, I had to make this right with Ed," Jamie tried to say respectfully as he removed the bloody T-shirt and pants he was wearing.

"Hey, Maggie, cut him some slack," I interjected. Because he was right. Clipping enemies was what we're about. This was a part of gang life.

"Ed, I don't need you to tell me what gang life is about. I was in that shit growing up, so don't come at me like I don't know what time it is. All I'm saying is why broadcast that shit on FaceTime? I don't want to hear my son murdering someone. I don't wanna see my only child as a monster. And on top of that, allow Khloé to see it too? What if she goes to the cops and tells 'em what she saw?"

"Come on now, Maggie, don't talk like that. You know my family is thorough. Especially my niece." I wasn't about to let her disrespect my niece like that.

"That didn't stop her from ratting the guys who did that murder. She even talked about it on the fucking news!" Maggie pointed out.

"Is this how you've been feeling the entire time?" I asked, turning my attention directly towards her. "Is that where Jamie got that shit from? Because he never talked shit about Khloé until recently," I continued, and waited for her to answer.

"No, I didn't get it from her," Jamie blurted out. He made it obvious that he wanted us to stop arguing.

"Come on now, Jamie, do you think that I was born yesterday?" I cut him off and looked back at Maggie.

"So, tell me, Maggie. Tell me how you really feel," I pressed her.

"I'm done with this," she said and stormed away.

"What are you done with?" I asked her while following her to the kitchen. I wasn't gonna let her get away from me that easy, especially not since she wouldn't answer my question.

"Ed, just leave me alone because I'm done with this conversation," she said nonchalantly, and started washing the dishes that we'd used earlier in the day.

"Why didn't you tell me this sooner?"

"Because it wouldn't have made a difference."

"Yes, it would've."

"Ed, it wouldn't have mattered and you know it to be true. I mean, you walk around here bragging about her all the time.

You talk about her being on TV, and then she got that award in LA. I mean, you wouldn't shut up. So that's why I didn't say anything. I'd rather come home to peace than a whole bunch of tension and discord."

I stood there and watched her while she washed and dried the dishes. Seeing her hurt like this made me feel fucked up on the inside. I loved this woman. I didn't want her walking around her house all screwed up in the head. I needed to make this right. Show her how much I loved and appreciated her. Now don't get it twisted, I loved my family too, so I was gonna have to figure out how to separate the two so that I didn't make one or the other feel slighted.

After Maggie and I talked, Jamie walked by us carrying his bloody clothes in his hands. "I know you're taking that shit out of here, right?" Maggie confronted him.

"Yeah, that's what I'm about to do now, after I get a plastic bag from the kitchen."

"Take them to Walt's crib. He's got a metal barrel in the backyard of this house. Tell 'im I sent you and he'll burn them up for you."

"A'ight. Cool!"

22

MAKING A DUMMY MOVE—KHLOÉ

I can't believe that I've been sitting out here at Frances's house for a little more than an hour and this hoe ain't here. I even called her cell phone several times and she didn't answer it. "You know what? Fuck it!" I mumbled and cranked up the ignition. As soon as I was about to turn on my headlights, my cell phone rang. I immediately looked at it and noticed it was Frances calling me back. I answered the call before it rang a second time. "Hello," I said.

"Hey, is everything all right?" she wanted to know. I knew she was referring to the many times I called her phone and she didn't answer it.

"I wanted to touch base with you. Are you home?"

"Yes, I was asleep, that's why I didn't get your call," she lied while trying to sound like she had just awakened. And on top of that, the bitch wasn't home. Her car was nowhere in sight. The lights in her place were all off too.

"Well, I went out tonight. Didn't see anything. I'm thinking they didn't have to go to work tonight," I commented, hoping she'd take the bait.

"Maybe they were put on a different assignment tonight. You know sometimes that happens. Cops call in all the time, and when they don't, the lieutenant would get another narcotics officer to shadow them when they go into the field. That used to happen to Ryan, I mean Gavin, all the time," she explained. And boy, did I hear her slip up and call Ryan's name. I knew she wanted to kick herself in the butt for mistakenly doing that. I knew she was also wondering if I caught it or not. Aside from that, she had never been so casual and understanding about me not being able to give her an update. *What's up with this chick?*

Before I could attempt to figure about what was going on, I saw a car coming from behind me. I watched it from my rearview mirror. The closer the car got, it became clearer that it was Frances's car. "So, what do you want me to do?" I asked her.

"Where are you?" she wanted to know. I saw she wanted to play cat-and-mouse games with me, and I wasn't in the mood for that. So I purposely, and in an indirect way, let her know that I didn't hear her utter Ryan's name. As a matter of fact, I wouldn't mention it at all.

"I just got home. If you would've answered my call earlier, I would've met you at a coffee shop or somewhere," I added, and by the time I closed my mouth, she pulled up and drove her car into her designated parking space, which was three cars back from where I was parked.

"Oh, it's fine. I had one of those days where I just wanted to relax. The baby has been kicking and tossing and turning all day it seems." She kept talking. "Well, look, let me call you back. I've gotta use the bathroom. So, give me about thirty minutes. If you don't hear from me, then I'll call you in the morning."

"Okay, sounds great," I told her and then we ended our call.

Immediately after we hung up, I grabbed my satellite device and pointed it directly at her car. After I powered it on, I heard two voices. I turned completely around in my seat, and that's when I saw both car doors open and out came Frances and Ryan. That dumb bitch lied to me once again. "Are you gonna call her back?" Ryan asked her.

"And say what? It's not like she's got something to tell me. You heard what she said. She wasn't able to spy on y'all tonight," Frances said as she and Ryan leaned up against the hood of her car.

"You need to be more focused on getting her to set up Brad and Chris. 'Cause if we don't get them out of the way, we're gonna have to split that money five ways."

"Wait, what do you mean, Brad and Chris? What happened to Nick?"

"He found out what we were doing, so he said that if I didn't keep him on he was going to blow the whistle to Brad."

"Fuck! Why didn't you tell me before?"

"We just talked about it an hour ago."

"So, what are we going to do now?" Frances asked him. She made it perfectly clear that she needed some answers.

"I've been thinking about this shit for a while. And planting drugs on them ain't gonna work. Going to Internal Affairs, like Gavin was going to do, will get us killed. And besides, if I dropped dime on them, they'd rat me out in return. So we're gonna kill 'em," Ryan said.

"Kill them? How do you propose we do that?"

"Call Khloé and tell her that she doesn't have to investigate Gavin's death because you found out that Brad and Chris did it. And because they were the ones that did it, you want her to get her uncle to do the job."

"Her uncle?"

"Yeah, homicide detectives are looking for him right now."

"For what?"

"That murder in Park Place. He shot and killed one of his own for disrespecting him. The dead guy's cousin got away. A relative of the dead guy called homicide and gave up the shooter's name. He agreed to go in and speak with them, but he hasn't done it yet."

"Damn, I wished that I had known this earlier. I could've used this against her."

"What do you mean? You can still use it."

"How?"

"I'll tell them that I got some intel on a bust. We all go to that spot, and Khloé's uncle and his goons can be waiting to ambush them."

"Ryan, that's an awesome idea, but she's not gonna go for that. And I'm almost certain that her uncle won't go for it either."

"Tell the cops to make the murder case go away and we'll pay him as well."

Frances paused for a moment and then she said, "I don't know, baby. I don't think that's gonna fly with Khloé. She doesn't seem like the type. I don't think I'm gonna be able to convince her to get her uncle and his gang members to help."

"Trust me, if you say that we'll give her uncle a get-out-of-jail-free card, she will do it."

Frances sighed heavily. "So, when are you planning this drug bust? She gonna have to give her uncle a time, especially if he agrees to do it, which of course I say that he won't."

"We've gotta have it done at least by six p.m. Because we gotta pick all those kids up by midnight. So that gives us a six-hour window to call for backup and go back to the precinct to do an interview with homicide and fill out some paperwork. If all goes according to plan, I could be out of there by ten. That's more than enough time for me to pick up the van and go and round up the cargo."

"I sure hope things work out the way you're saying it

will," Frances commented. "Hey, is that Brad pulling up?" She turned her focus to the car coming from behind us.

"Yep, that's him," Ryan replied, and then he stood completely up. "Give me a kiss," he said to Frances, and then he leaned in towards her.

"What time do you get off tonight?" she asked him after they kissed.

"Four a.m."

"Well, hello there," Brad greeted Frances from the driver's seat after he pulled up in an unmarked police vehicle.

"Hi, Brad," she replied.

"Wait, you're acting like you don't wanna see me," Brad commented and then he chuckled.

"Ahhh, leave her alone."

"If it wasn't for me, you two wouldn't be enjoying that bundle of joy in that belly," Brad added in a joking manner. But Frances clearly didn't find it all that funny.

"Babe, call me later tonight if you get a chance," Frances said, and then she started walking towards her house.

After Ryan got in the car, the car idled there until Frances went into her place. Seconds later, they drove away.

If I didn't get an earful today, then I don't know what to call it. I heard everything from Ryan advising Frances to enlist me to get my uncle Ed to kill Brad and Chris, to Ryan knowing about my uncle murdering the other guy. And to add another layer of scandal, Brad insinuated that it was him that got Gavin out of the way, which is the only reason why Ryan and Frances could be together. *Oh my God! I don't know what to do. Or what to say. What the fuck am I going to do now?*

I couldn't believe that I was able to get a night's worth of sleep last night, especially with everything that happened yesterday. My first thought was to hop in my car and head to my uncle's spot, but I blew the spot up last night when the cops realized who I was. So there was no way I could go over there and tell him what I heard last night. What I might have to do was do a FaceTime with him. I'm not sure if the cops could wiretap that—but then, who knows?

Surprisingly, Frances didn't call me last night, but she did call me this morning while I was in the shower. I called her back after I dried off and slipped on a robe. "Hey, Frances, you called?" I started off saying.

"Yes, how are you?" she replied.

"I'm fine. Thanks for asking," I told her, but I was feeling the exact opposite. I wanted to tell her to cut the crap and stop acting like she really cared about how I was doing.

"Okay, there's been some changes," she willed herself to say. I could tell that she was grappling with how to break the news to me that she didn't want me investigating her late husband's death. One side of me wanted to tell the dumb bitch to spit it out, while the other side of me wanted to tell her that I already knew what she was about to tell me.

"I'm all ears," I replied and became radio silent.

"I found out what really happened to my husband and who was behind it," she finally uttered, her words barely audible.

"No way. Really?" I replied, wanting to sound surprised.

"Yes, really."

"What happened?"

"I can't say over the phone, but I will say that I want to avenge my late husband's death and I'm gonna need some help doing it."

"Can you at least give me a hint? I'm dying to know over here."

"I can't. And I know you're against meeting me in public, but if you could make an exception just this one time, I could meet you and tell you everything. There's even more money on the table too," she reasoned.

I hesitated for a moment, even though I already knew the answer to her request. I was more interested in hearing her beg me then anything else. Oh, and the fact that she pulled out the money card was hilarious. In my mind, I'm like *Bitch, I see your whole hand, so stop acting like you're sweetening the pot, if you will.*

"How much money are we talking?" I played along.

"A lot."

"What's a lot?" I tried pressuring her to give me more information. But she wouldn't budge.

"If you meet me this morning, I will lay everything out and I will have more money for you, just in case you say yes."

I sighed heavily. "Okay, I will meet you."

"Great. Let's meet in an hour?"

"As soon as possible, I guess," I said, acting naïve.

"We could meet up at the Norfolk Outlets, get a hotdog and act like we're shopping," she suggested.

"Cool! Let's do that."

"Perfect. See you in an hour."

I tried desperately to will myself to appear calm when I met up with Frances. I couldn't afford to let her see me in this state, because I was truly in some shit, right now. I went from agreeing to help Frances investigate her husband's death to agreeing to meet her and discuss getting my uncle off the hook for that murder in exchange for his freedom. What was this world coming to?

As planned, I met Frances at the Norfolk Outlets. When I pulled into the parking lot, I found her sitting in her car on the food court side of this massive shopping center. She smiled at me when our eyes connected. I smiled back, but I wasn't in a cheerful mood. "You wanted to meet me here because you're hungry, huh?" I commented. I wanted to display a cool and calm temperament.

She smiled. "Can't you tell?" she replied as she rubbed her pregnant belly.

"Yes, I can," I teased her. "So, how far along are you?" I continued. Up until now, I never questioned her about her personal life. But I did today, because I would never have that chance again.

"Twenty-nine weeks," she said.

She saw me trying to calculate the numbers in my head as we walked towards the building, and chuckled. "I'm a little over seven months."

I forced myself to smile. "Okay, thank you for that."

"You're welcome," she replied, and then she looked up and gazed at the sky.

"Think he's looking down on you?" I interrupted her thoughts.

"Who?" she wondered aloud. But then she caught herself once again slipping. "Who, my husband?" she asked, after realizing that she caused another blunder for herself. I didn't mention it either.

"Yes."

"I'm sure he is," she said, and then she lifted her right hand and started dabbing her tear ducts like she was trying to hold back tears. I swear, this bitch needed an Academy Award.

I fed her act. "Oh, I'm sorry. I don't wanna see you cry."

"Oh no, it's okay. I do need to get out sometimes because if I keep all this hurt bottled up inside, I could probably have a meltdown."

"You're right. So, are you having a girl or boy?" I kept the questions going.

"A boy."

"Figured out a name yet?"

"Yep, his name is going to be Reynolds."

"Why Reynolds?"

"It's Gavin's father's name," she said proudly. But I knew the bitch was lying. According to Social Security documents, Ryan's birth name is Reynold Ryan Lopez, but on his police file it's listed as R. Ryan Lopez. So once again, this tramp is telling me yet another lie.

When we entered the food court, we both decided on getting a personal-size pizza, and then we found a table in the corner next to a window. This way we could see who was coming or going. Frances didn't know this, but after we were handed our food, I allowed her to walk in front of me so I could power on my cell phone recorder. I needed all the audio and footage I could get, just in case this tramp tried to come for me later.

"This pizza looks so good."

"Yes, it does," I agreed as I layered it with grated Parmesan. "So, tell me who killed your husband?" I got to the point. The battery life on my cell phone was half full, so I needed to get this show on the road before the battery died.

"Brad and Chris did it. My husband had some dirt on them and threatened to go to Internal Affairs, so they killed him."

"Well, if you know this, then why don't you go to Internal Affairs?"

"Brad and Chris are some very dangerous men. If they murdered my husband and he was their partner, then what do you think they would do to me?"

"How did you find out this information?"

"I promised my source that I wouldn't divulge their name."

"Okay, so what's up with this proposition you said you had for me but that you couldn't talk about over the phone?"

"Your uncle Ed is in a gang, right?"

"He used to be, why?" I asked her, trying to play the naïve role.

"Well, I heard that he still is."

"From who?"

"It doesn't matter. But he's still connected, right?"

"I'll have to find out," I commented, giving her a hard time. I didn't want her to think that my uncle was easy access.

"Well, you do that, because I will pay him and whoever he can get to take Brad and Chris out."

"You mean, kill?" I questioned her. Once again having her to believe that I was shocked that we were having this conversation.

"Yes, kill. I want Brad and Chris to pay for what they did to my husband. And if they can handle that for me, I will pay him and whoever else ten thousand dollars for Brad's head and Chris's head."

"Oh my goodness! Are you serious?" I widened my eyes in fake shock.

"Yes, I am serious," she said confidently.

"Frances, I'm sure that you're hurting, but I can't get involved with that. I am not going to prison for the rest of my life because I helped you facilitate two murder hits. I'm just not that kind of person," I told her, and then I took a bite from my slice of pizza.

"Is it the money? Because I told you that I could give you more too. I can give you twenty thousand. So, I'm giving you twenty, your uncle twenty, and the other person twenty also," she expressed. She was not letting this go.

"Frances, it's not even about the money. I just don't want any blood on my hands."

"Okay, well, put me in contact with your uncle. Or one of the other gang members."

"Frances, that still makes me involved."

"I can make your uncle's murder charges go away," she blurted out. I could tell that this last-ditch effort was pulled from her gut.

Once again, I played naïve. "What murder charges?"

"My source knows that your uncle shot and killed that dude Apple Head because he disrespected you. Now I can make any and all the evidence go away if your uncle does this job. He can get paid a lot of money for his work and become an innocent man all in the same twenty-four hours."

I sat there and watched Frances as she pulled all this bull-shit from her hat. She was a bold chick. If I was an innocent bystander sitting in this pizza place watching her talk to me, I wouldn't believe that she was talking to me about killing two narcotics police detectives. This bitch was vicious.

"So, what will it be?" She pressed the issue. *She ain't letting up*.

"What's gonna happen if my uncle doesn't do it?" I asked, testing her.

"My source is going to make sure that when he finally gets picked up, that he will never see the light of day again," she replied candidly.

"When does this need to be done? Because when I go to him with this proposal, he gonna want to know when you want this job done."

"Tonight."

"Tonight? That's too soon."

"I'm sorry, but it needs to be done."

"Well, I can tell you now that my uncle isn't gonna be able to do it. But if he gets a couple guys from his organization to do it, will he still be able to get the get-out-of-jail-free card?"

"As long as this mission is done, yes, I was told with the utmost sincerity that that murder investigation will go away."

I took a deep breath and then I exhaled. "Okay, let me make a call," I said, and then I got up from the table. I walked to the far end of the restaurant so she wouldn't be able to hear my conversation when I talked to my uncle Ed.

"Hey, Uncle Ed, I really need to talk to you," I whispered.

There was a white couple a few feet away from me, so I couldn't risk them hearing what I was about to say.

"What's up, baby girl?"

"I've got a job for you, but you may need to outsource it."

"What kind of job is it?"

"I can't say right now. But I will say that it's paying forty grand and a get-out-of-jail-free card."

"No fucking way?" he commented with excitement.

"Yes, way," I said nonchalantly. I couldn't afford to let Frances see me get excited with my uncle.

"So, when am I gonna hear about this job?"

"That's what I was going to ask you. Because I know that you can't leave the house. And if I come back there, I will be making your spot hot."

Uncle Ed went silent for a moment and then he said, "FaceTime me on Maggie's cell phone. Her line is good. It ain't never been compromised. Do you have her number?"

"No, what is it?"

"It's 757-555-1091."

"Okay, I'm saving it in my phone now," I told him and took my cell phone from my ear and saved it under "Forty Grand."

"So, when are you gonna call me?"

"I'm at this pizza spot, so I'm gonna go in the bathroom and call you in a second."

"A'ight, I'll be waiting."

Immediately after I ended the call with my uncle, I turned my attention towards Frances, held up one of my fingers and mouthed the words *I'll be right back*. She understood what I meant and gave me a head nod.

When I entered the bathroom, I checked every stall to see if I was alone, and when I realized that I was, I dialed Maggie's cell phone number through FaceTime and waited for my uncle to answer. He answered after only three rings. His face looked cheerful and bright. If I had murder charges looming over my head, I wouldn't be smiling at all. I'd be finding a way to leave town and never come back.

"Whatcha got for me?" he asked.

"Is Maggie around?" I whispered so that no one outside of the bathroom door could hear me, and I also did it so that Maggie couldn't hear me either.

"I'm in our bedroom. She's in the kitchen talking to Jamie."

"Okay, well, check it out. Remember yesterday when I told you that chick Frances was going to ask me to stop working that bogus-ass mission she had me on?"

"Yeah."

"Well, she just did it. We're at this pizza spot in Virginia Beach. So, after we get our food, we sit down, start eating, and that's when she says to me that she wants me to stop working because she knows who offed her husband."

"Did she tell you who did it?"

"Yes, she threw the narc police Brad and Chris underneath the bus. Talking about her husband was being hounded by Internal Affairs and he threatened to blow the whistle on all of them, so they had to shut his mouth up for good."

"So, how much is she paying to have this done?"

"She said she's paying twenty K per cop."

Uncle Ed chuckled, but not too loud, so that Maggie and Jamie wouldn't hear him. "That's forty bands."

"Yep, it sure is."

"Where the fuck is she getting that kind of money from?"

"See, that's the thing. Something is gonna happen tonight where she's gonna get a lot of money after they deliver some cargo, but I just don't know what that is. But I do know that they want Brad and Chris gone so that they can keep their portion of the money."

"Oh, so she's telling you that she wants those two cops

dead because they killed her husband, but in reality, they want them eliminated because they don't want to give them their bread."

"Exactly."

"So what's this get-out-of-jail-free card she's talking about?"

"Well, she and that fucking cop Ryan know that you were the one that murdered that guy. And I know she's not lying, because when I was staking out her house out last night, I heard him say out of his own mouth that the cops in homicide got word that you killed that guy. Apparently, someone from Bullet's family called in, gave them your name, and promised to go there and have a talk about how the murder went down, but as of right now, he hasn't showed up."

"And he ain't gonna show up either. Ol' bitch-ass nigga! Man, I swear, I don't know how that dude got in our organization. He was a rat from the start."

"Well, never mind all of that, because what's done is done. He said that if you do the job, the evidence will disappear."

"What evidence do they have? It ain't like I left DNA behind. And the dude that snitched me out is dead. So he's gonna have to come harder than that."

"So, what do you want me to do? She's waiting at the table for me to come back with an answer."

"So, when does she want it done?"

"Tonight."

"Tonight! That's impossible. I can't even leave the house right now."

"I told her that, but she knows that you're in the Ace of Spades and said that if you can't do it, then have one of the other members do it."

"Damn! She's a beast! She doesn't care who pulls the trigger. Just as long as it gets done, huh?"

"That's what it seems like."

Uncle Eddie fell silent for three to four seconds and then he said, "I wonder what's in that cargo she and that cop is talking about."

"I wondered the same thing. Whatever it is, they're picking it up and delivering it to someone that's gonna pay them a lot of money for it."

"Did she tell you where she wanted the job done? I mean, this thing needs to be executed right. My boys don't do sloppy jobs," my uncle boasted.

I wanted to remind him that he did a sloppy job when he killed Bullet's cousin, but I decided against it. Now wasn't the time or place. "She and I haven't gotten that far. I told her that I was going to ask you if the whole thing was possible."

"I'll tell you what, tell her that if she gives me fifty K, I'll get my boys to do it. And then we'll go from there with where and how. And when you call me back, call me on Maggie's cell phone again. Also, check her to make sure she's not wired. I don't want you mixed up in that shit, especially if I get some of our troopers to do the job."

"Okay. I will, and I'll call you in a bit," I assured him.

Instead of going back to the table, I called Frances and told her to meet me in the restroom. She walked in the restroom less than fifty seconds later. She gave me a look of hope. "So, what did he say?"

"Take off your jacket and lift your shirt," I instructed her.

She looked at me like she was appalled by my request. "I need to make sure that this conversation isn't being recorded," I told her.

"I'm not wired," she assured me.

"I'm sure you're not. But I've got a lot to lose, so I've got to be careful," I insisted as I took a couple of steps towards her. It only took a few seconds for her to realize that I wasn't playing games with her. She sucked her teeth, took her jacket off, placed it across the baby-changing table, and then she lifted her shirt. I looked at her belly, and her baby bump was huge. Her stomach looked like it was about to burst.

My instructions continued. "Turn around." When she turned around, I patted her down from front to back and from her neck to her ankles. Once I felt like I checked her thoroughly, I stood up and stepped back.

"Did you find anything?" she asked sarcastically as she slipped her jacket back on.

"You can never be too sure," I commented.

"So, what's the verdict?" she wanted to know.

"He said that he could arrange to have it done for fifty thousand."

"Okay, I can do that," she replied. "Did you tell him that I need it done tonight?"

"Yes, he knows it. So, he wants to get some additional information so he can plan the whole thing accordingly."

"Can I speak with him?"

I hesitated for a moment because I wasn't sure if it would be a good idea to call my uncle back, especially via FaceTime. So I went with audio calling instead. I used Maggie's number instead of his. "Why didn't you FaceTime me?"

"Because I have Frances with me. She wanted to talk to you."

"A'ight, put her on," my uncle said.

I handed Frances my cell phone, but I took it off speakerphone first. When she had my cell phone in hand, she pressed it to her ear. "Hello," she said timidly. But I couldn't hear my uncle's reply. I was able to follow the conversation through Frances's questions and answers.

"I was thinking, since they're known for kicking in drug houses and taking drugs and money from the dealers, you could get a couple of guys to wait in ambush at one of their drug houses. My late husband told me how his bosses would beat the guys up, take their money, and sometimes wouldn't arrest them. Now I don't know how you view the two guys

I'm talking about, but I want their dirty ass off the streets because they took the man that meant the world to me," she expressed, and then she fell silent.

I guess this was the time when my uncle asked when was he gonna get the money, because she told him that she'd give him half up front and the rest when the job was done. "How am I going to know where you need them to go?" she added, and then she paused.

My uncle uttered a few more words and then she thanked him. "He wants to talk to you," she said and handed me my cell phone.

"Hello," I said.

"Hey, baby girl, check it out, she's gonna give you half of the dough now, and when she does, I want you to call me and I'll tell you what time and the location of the spot where we're gonna do the job so that you can pass it on to her."

"Okay, I'll call you back in a bit," I agreed knowing that he and I was about to make a ton of money once this job is done.

After my uncle and I ended the call I looked at Frances and said, "Are you ready?"

"As ready as I'll ever be.

23

THE SET UP!—UNCLE ED

Under normal circumstances, I would be gearing up to do the job Frances wanted me to do. But I'm cool with it because I'm taking half of the bounty and I'm adding a finder's fee to it. Yep, I'm about to get a nice-size payout and won't have to lift a finger. Like the rapper Future said, "Life Is Good"!

I didn't waste a second getting on the phone with Tommy Boy since he was the head of our organization now. It was out of respect that he was briefed on any and all jobs executed on his watch. He also got a cut of the bounty as well. That was one of the laws within our gang.

I called him on his latest burner cell phone and he took the call immediately. "You must got some money news for me," he said cheerfully.

"You know it."

"So, how can I help you today?"

"Remember I was telling you that my niece got hired by that chick whose husband was a narc and supposedly committed suicide?"

"Yeah, I remember. What about it?"

"Well, she found out who killed dude and wants to hire us to take out two cops that did it."

"How much she paying?"

"Thirty grand," I lied. There was no reason for him to know exactly what the cost of the bounty was. Shit, I was the one who was taking all the risks. I mean, I was setting this whole operation up.

"When does she want it done?"

"Tonight."

"Are you gonna get your hands dirty?"

"Nah, you know I can't show my face on the streets until those crackers find homeboy's body. So I was thinking we could put Peanut, Ty-Ty and Jay on it. We could pay 'em three grand each and they'll take care of it."

"Yeah, you're right. They'll definitely take care of it."

"Are they at the spot with you, right now?"

"Yep, they're here. You wanna talk to one of 'em?"

"Yeah, put Ty-Ty on the phone."

"A'ight, hold on," Tommy Boy said, and then the line went radio silent. Less than a minute later, Ty-Ty spoke. "What's up, Ed? I just heard that you need me."

"Yeah, I do. I got a job for you, Jay, and Peanut."

"Cool. Where do you need for us to go?"

"Is that house on Lexington Street still a shooting gallery?"

"Yeah."

"A'ight, cool. I want you to clear out all the dope fiends and set it up for a sting. Remember those narcs that run up in spots and take dude's work and they money and put it in their pockets?"

"Yeah, I know who those crackers are."

"A'ight, cool. 'Cause I got two of them coming through thinking that they're doing a sting, but y'all niggas are gonna crucify they asses after they kick in the crib."

"Word!" Ty-Ty said eagerly.

"Word! And y'all dudes are getting three grand each for the job."

"Man, you just don't know how much this is going to help me. My girl is pregnant. And now I can get all this stuff she needs."

"I'm glad I can help. So, get Peanut and Jay ready because this is going to happen around five to six o'clock this evening. Do you have a burner phone?"

"Yes, and I just got it today too."

"Give the number to me," I instructed him. After I programmed that cell phone number in my phone, I told him I would hit him up later with the final details.

"Think this will be a good hit?" Tommy Boy asked me after Ty-Ty gave him the phone back.

"We'll see. Khloé's getting the first half of the dough now. So, as soon as I get word that she got the money then I'm gonna call Ty-Ty back so we can put the final touches on the sting."

"Okay, but you stay off the grid until everything blows over."

"You know I'm already on it."

When I ended my call with Tommy Boy, I left the bedroom and headed back in the kitchen. Maggie was washing dishes and Jamie was gone. "Where's Jamie?" I asked her.

"I think he went next door to Lily's apartment."

"He better leave her alone before she traps his ass and becomes pregnant. She already has about ten of 'em running around the parking lot and getting in trouble."

Maggie chuckled. "She does not have ten kids."

"Well, it seems like it."

"Never mind them, I heard bits and pieces of your phone call to Khloé and that lady she put on the phone. And all I'm gonna say is be careful. Killing guys in the street is one thing, but to order contracts on cops is something entirely different.

Yesterday it was the guy you shot in broad daylight. Then it was the cousin of that guy you shot. Now you're fucking with cops. Judges give out life sentences for that shit. They also give out death penalties too."

"I understand what you're saying, and you're right. But I'm not the one getting my hands dirty. Me and Tommy Boy recruited three dudes to do it. So I'm good."

"I hope so," she said nonchalantly, but I hadn't convinced her enough. She'll see, though.

While she and I continued to chop it up, Lily started frantically knocking on our front door, and then she opened it when she realized that it was unlocked. "Maggie, the cops are harassing Jamie," she told us.

I was instantly pissed off because I couldn't go outside to help him. Maggie dropped everything she was doing and raced down the flight of stairs and into the parking lot entrance where Jamie was being held by the cops. I got a bird's-eye view from the front room window.

I couldn't hear what Maggie was saying, but her body language spoke volumes. She went from getting in the face of one of the two cops while the other cop had Jamie sitting on the curb handcuffed. I watched as Maggie went toe to toe with one cop, and then she turned her focus towards the second cop. After about ten minutes of back-and-forth, both cops finally uncuffed Jamie and let him go with Maggie. I watched as Maggie threw a tantrum the entire way back to the apartment while Jamie walked alongside of her. At one point I chuckled because I knew that my woman was a firecracker and I was sure they were saying the same thing.

"Where did Lily go?" Maggie asked me as soon as she walked back in the apartment.

"I guess she went home," I replied. "So, what happened? Why was they messing with you?" I asked Jamie after he reappeared.

"They said I had a warrant. And I told them that I didn't. But they handcuffed me anyway and ran my name in their system. And while I was waiting for them to tell me that I could go, the cop that handcuffed me asked me where you were. And that they know that you live in this building. So I told them if they know you live here, then go and get a warrant and stop harassing me, but they wasn't trying to hear me. Oh, and I think they asked Lily if she knew you. But I don't know what she said though," Jamie explained.

"Is that why you asked me where she went?" I directed my question to Maggie.

"Yep, that's exactly why I asked you," she replied.

"Go to her crib and tell her to come here," I instructed Maggie.

"I'll be right back," she said, and then she left the apartment.

Jamie sat down on the sofa. "You a'ight?" I asked him.

"When they ran up on me, I thought they were fucking with me because of Bullet's murder. But when they started asking questions about you, I knew they didn't know anything about it."

"What did they say about me?"

"They said that they know that you killed Apple Head and that they're gonna find you. But if you wanna save yourself from embarrassment, then you should turn yourself in."

I chuckled. "Come on now, do they know who they're dealing with? Real OGs don't turn themselves in to the cops. They're out of their damn minds."

Jamie laughed. "I know, I was thinking the same thing when they said it."

"Did you hear what they said to Lily?"

"Not really. But I did hear one of the cops say something about reward money."

Before I could ask Jamie another question, Maggie and

Lily walked back in the apartment. I zoomed in on Lily's face and noticed that she looked kind of nervous, and I hadn't even opened my mouth yet. "Lily, tell Eddie what you just told me," Maggie instructed her.

"When Jamie was walking towards my front door, I was coming out with my trash in my hand so I could take it to the dumpster. Jamie took the trash out of my hand so he could take it downstairs to the parking lot himself. Right after he put the trash in the dumpster, the police walked up on him and asked him what his name was. And that's when Jamie told them that he didn't have to give them shit because he's standing outside where he lives at and he ain't bothering nobody. So the fat short cop told him that he had a big mouth and since he wasn't cooperating with them, they were gonna detain him until they found out who he was. So I yelled at them and told 'em his first name, but they thought I was lying so they handcuffed him and made him sit on the curb."

Maggie coached her on. "Tell 'em what the cop said to you right before you came here to tell us they had Jamie."

"The other cop pulled me to the side and asked me have I known you and seen you these last couple of days," Lily said as she looked directly at me.

"What did you tell 'em?" I wanted to know.

"I told him that I knew you but I haven't seen you in a while."

"Did you tell 'em where I live?" I continued to question her.

"No," she said. But she hesitated, so I knew she was lying.

"Lily, that's not what you told me," Maggie blurted out.

"What did she tell you?" I wondered aloud, speaking to Maggie. Lily was talking too slow for me and it was beginning to frustrate the hell out of me too.

"She told me that they asked her did you live in this apartment with me. And she told me that she said yes. So they said that if she saw you again, to give them a call because she could get some reward money," Maggie explained.

"Did you tell 'em that you'll call 'em?"

"No." Her words were barely audible.

"Lily, are you lying to me?" I pressed her. I needed to know how I was going to move around to avoid running into those cops.

"No, I'm telling you the truth," she tried to convince me.

I looked at Jamie. "What do you think?"

"I don't know. If she did, I didn't hear it," Jamie said.

"Ed, they don't know where you at. I put that on my kids," she insisted.

I hesitated for a second, looking at Lily's body language. She was on edge and her expression showed it. "Go head and leave. If they come at you again and ask you any more questions about me, let Maggie know, all right?" I told her.

"Okay. I will," she replied and then she shot out the front door.

After she left, I looked at Maggie and Jamie and asked them what were their thoughts.

"I don't trust her. And I think she told them that you live here," Maggie pointed out.

"You think so?"

"Yes, I do. So, keep your eyes on her."

"A'ight," he replied.

24

GEARING UP!—KHLOÉ

Frances instructed me to follow her to the bank. But I waited outside in my car until she came back with the money my uncle Eddie demanded. She returned with three stacks of one-hundred-dollar bills and handed them to me. Two of the stacks were wrapped in ten-thousand-dollar paper strips, and the third stack was wrapped in a five-thousand-dollar strip. "Are you gonna make the call to your uncle now? We need to get this show on the road."

"Let me call him now," I said.

Frances stood next to my car while I dialed Maggie's cell phone number. Uncle Eddie answered. "Everything good?" he asked me. He sounded more anxious than she was.

"Yes, she just gave me the twenty-five grand. I have it on me right now."

"A'ight, let me speak with her."

I handed Frances my cell phone. But this time I put it on speaker so that I could hear it too.

"Hello," she said.

"Hey, so this is what I want you to do," he started off.

"Have those dudes go to 310 Lexington Avenue in Huntersville at four thirty. We gon' make it look like we selling drugs on the front porch. And then we're gonna run in the house so they can follow us."

"Don't forget you're only gonna do away with two of them, right?"

"Yeah, I know. The tall white dude with the full beard and the guy with the blond hair. Brad and Chris, right?"

"Yeah, that's the two."

"Immediately after everything is done, I expect to get the rest of the money," my uncle reminded her.

"Oh, no problem. I have it right now," she replied eagerly. She just didn't know that she shouldn't have let that cat out of the bag. If my uncle was in front of her at this very moment, she would've been robbed. No questions asked.

"Since you have the money now, why don't you give it to my niece. That way we don't have to see each other again," he added.

"No, I'll feel much better if I hold on to it until the job is done."

"Okay, if that's the way you wanna do it. I'm just giving you options," my uncle said.

"I can appreciate that. So, do I need to do anything on my part?"

"All you need to do is have your cop friend direct his boys to that spot on Lexington Avenue and we'll do the rest."

"Four thirty, right?"

"Yep. Four thirty."

"Okay, thank you."

"Yeah, a'ight. You just have the rest of my money on hand once my boys do their job."

"Will do. You have my word."

I ended my call with my uncle after I told him that I would wait for him to call me back after the job was done. And before she walked away to get back in her car, she thanked me for facilitating this hit. "So, when do I get my part?" I asked her.

"Oh, I completely forgot," she said, and then she reached down in her purse. She pulled out a ten-thousand-dollar stack of one-hundred-dollar bills and handed it to me.

"I thought I was getting twenty thousand," I reminded her.

"I'll give you the other half when the job is completed," she replied.

I stuffed the money in my purse and told her that we'd talk soon. I watched her as she got in her car and drove away. All I could do was shake my head in disgust, thinking about how she came up with this elaborate scheme to cash in on a lot of money and kill people in the process. She was a treacherous bitch. But I was street-smart, and that would take me further than she could ever imagine.

I called my uncle Eddie back after I drove away from the bank. This time I FaceTimed him on Maggie's cell phone. "Did she really give you twenty-five grand?"

"Yep, she sure did." I lifted the money up to the cell phone just enough so he could see it.

"How are you feeling right now?" he wanted to know.

"I guess I'm feeling all right," I replied, not really knowing how to answer the question.

"Think she's gonna go through with it?"

"Yes, you should've seen her face after she gave me the money. I believe if you could do the job now, she would be all-in."

"I just got off the phone with my boys and they're ready to go."

"Are you sure that they know exactly who to eliminate?"

"Yeah, they know." And then he went into detail about

how this mission was going to go down. While he and I were going back and forth, I heard loud noises in the background and so did my uncle. It sounded chaotic. *Boom!* I watched my uncle as he turned around in the direction of his bedroom door.

"Get down on the floor now!" someone yelled.

Startled by the immediate uproar, anxiety consumed me when I realized that a SWAT team bum-rushed his apartment to arrest him. Before I could stay anything, one of the cops wearing black combat gear with the word *SWAT* engraved on his bullet-proof vest picked up Maggie's cell phone from the floor and looked in the screen. Our eyes met. "Oh, so Mr. Mercer knows the local news lady," he commented, and then he tapped another cop on the arm and bragged about my uncle Eddie knowing me. "Hey, Karl, check this out. He knows the news lady," he continued as he turned the cell phone around.

"Yeah, I know. She's his niece," the other cop said.

"Well, sorry, niece. We're taking him downtown and booking him on murder charges," the same cop announced.

"You don't have shit on him! He hasn't killed anyone!" I roared through the phone.

"Tell that to the judge," the cop said, and then he ended the call.

I sat there in my car, overwhelmed and consumed with fear. How the fuck did they know that he was in the apartment? I told the cops that I encountered that he didn't live there. I guess they didn't believe me. And now I felt guilty that I brought that heat to his place. To make matters worse, how was I supposed to move forward with the plans that myself and Ed set up? *Damn! Ugh! What am I going to do now?*

My first and only thought was to drive over to his apartment to see what exactly was going on. I could talk to Maggie and find out.

On my way to my uncle and Maggie's apartment, which was across town, I was beginning to feel like I was having a panic attack. This couldn't be going on right now. I had too much at stake. Something had to give. I needed my uncle on the streets, not in jail.

I put the pedal to the metal and arrived to my uncle's apartment in less than twelve minutes. But by the time I arrived, he was handcuffed in the back seat of a regular police car. I tried to get into the parking lot of the building, but it was blocked by a slew of Suburban SUVs and unmarked detective cars.

I finally found a place to park my car, and as soon as I powered off the ignition, I hopped out of the driver seat and bolted towards the apartment building. Maggie was standing outside her apartment with her son Jamie by her side. I called her name and as soon as she heard my voice, she looked in my direction. "Come up here!" she shouted.

"Okay," I replied, and walked over to the flight of steps. Before I could put my foot on the first step, a uniformed cop refused to let me get by him. "Do you live in this building?" he asked me.

"No, I don't, but my aunt does. Didn't you just hear her tell me to come upstairs?" I replied sarcastically.

"If you don't live in this building, then you can't go past this point."

I instantly got frustrated. "Are you serious right now?"

"I'm afraid I am."

I stood ten feet back from the police officer and called out Maggie's name. "This cop down here won't let me come upstairs!" I shouted to her.

"I'll be down there as soon as these fuckers get out my house!" she shouted back.

"Just send Jamie down here!" I shouted.

"Okay," she said, and then I saw Jamie walking away from Maggie and he headed downstairs to meet me.

When Jamie got within three feet of me, I went into question mode. "So, what happened?"

"They kicked my mom's front door open, talking about they had an arrest warrant for him because somebody told them that he killed that dude Apple Head. But when they came in there, I thought that they was coming there for that guy Bullet's murder. Man, I was scared as shit," Jamie explained.

"I saw him sitting in the back of that police car," I stated as I pointed towards a patrol car near the entryway of the parking lot.

"Think they know anything about it?"

"Maybe not. Because if they did, they would've dropped both names."

"Think they got a case since one of the dudes is dead?"

"I don't think so, because they'll need testimony from one of the victims to get a conviction. Unless someone from that neighborhood comes forward."

"Nah, that ain't gonna ever happen. Ain't nobody crazy enough to do that."

"Well, then there you have it," I commented, and then I changed the subject. "Did Eddie tell you about the job we had set up?" I whispered loud enough for him to hear me.

"Nah, but I can find out."

"Well, you can't ask him because he's in police custody. You're gonna have to talk to Tommy Boy. As a matter of fact, I'm gonna need you to take me to him."

"A'ight, let me make sure my mom is straight before I leave."

"Absolutely."

The cops hung around for another thirty minutes and left when they searched every inch of Maggie's apartment. Apparently they were searching her apartment to find the weapon that killed Apple Head. Unfortunately for them, they didn't find it. "They didn't have to tear up my apartment like they did. They were so freaking nasty. I was so glad when you pulled up, because if Jamie would've hung around the front door, he would've gotten arrested too," Maggie told me when I finally got upstairs.

"Ma, I couldn't stand around and let them crackers talk to me the way they were doing without me saying something back."

"They were pushing your buttons so that they could arrest you too. I'm just so glad that Eddie didn't have any guns hidden around the apartment," Maggie said.

"Me too. Because they could've been nasty and locked you up too," I told her.

"Or even me," Jamie added.

"Think they might give him a bond?" Maggie wanted to know.

"For murder? I don't think so. But if they do, it will be extremely high," I replied.

"How much is high?" Maggie's questions continued.

"Five hundred thousand. Maybe a million," I guessed.

"If it's that much, I know that I will never get him out."

"Look, I don't know if you know, but Eddie and I have been working a job. The job is supposed to happen this evening. This job will put fifty thousand dollars in his pocket and a get-out-of-jail-free card for the murder of that guy Apple Head. But in order for this job to move forward, I'm gonna need to speak with Tommy Boy."

"I told her that I'll take her as soon as the cops leave," Jamie interjected.

"How is he gonna get a get-out-of-jail-free card? Only cops, prosecutors, and judges do that, right?" Maggie wondered aloud.

"I don't have the specifics right now. But he's doing something for someone and they're gonna make sure whatever evidence the homicide detectives have will disappear."

"No way. Really?" Maggie said.

"Yes, really. Now I need to take Jamie with me so we can make a run," I pointed out.

"Where are you two going?" Maggie asked.

"Ma, it's best that you don't know. Just stay here and I'll be right back," Jamie said, and then he and I left the apartment.

Immediately after Jamie and I got into my car, I sped away and headed to the house run by Tommy Boy, one of Ace of Spades leaders. "I appreciate you doing this for me," I started off saying. I didn't want to take this drive all the way to Park Place in silence. It would be truly awkward.

"No problem. Looking out for each other is what family is supposed to do," Jamie stated.

"That's good to hear," I noted. "So, Ed didn't tell you about the job that he set up for later?" I asked him.

"Nah, he didn't. I've seen you and him talking a lot, but that's it."

I thought for a moment about whether it would be cool to tell Jamie about the job. Then I realized that he was going to find out anyway. So why make him wait? I took a deep breath and exhaled. "A woman reached out to me whose husband was a drug cop. She asked me to investigate his death. Now, the police report says that he committed suicide, but she believes that he was murdered by his cop buddies."

"Hey, wait, I heard about that. That cop's name was Gavin. He was a piece of shit. Him and the other narco cops is known for stealing dude's drug money, drugs, and they even took guns from a lot of dudes I know. And most of them didn't get arrested. Now don't get me wrong, I'd rather for a cop to take my money and drugs, but how would I explain to dudes that gave me the drugs, that the cops took my shit but I didn't get arrested? That shit ain't cool. I know a lot of niggas that got killed because of those cops. So I'm glad that motherfucker is dead," Jamie expressed.

"Well, Gavin's lady found out that he didn't kill himself, but that he was killed, so she wants the cops that did it, dead. So that's where Ed came in. He reached out to Tommy Boy and Tommy Boy gave him three guys that would pull off the job."

"Did Eddie give you the setup?"

"Yes, the cops that killed her husband will show up at the house on Lexington Avenue at four thirty, thinking that there's gonna be a big drug bust. Once they go inside, that's when they find out that they've been set up. The hit is for three of the four cops that's gonna show up. After the job is done, the guys who did the job will get paid."

"Shiiiit, why you ain't come to me? I got a team of soldiers that'll do that job. And for half of what you was gonna give Ed."

I thought for another moment, weighing the pros and cons of giving the job to Jamie versus having him take me to Tommy Boy and going forth with the guys that he and Ed had already assigned. "Okay, I'll tell you what, if you get at least one of the guys that Tommy Boy assigned to do the job, then I'm on board," I told him.

"Do you know any of the dudes' names that's supposed to do the job?"

"I remember a guy named Ty-Ty. It was supposed to be him and two other guys. I don't remember their names right now."

"A'ight, cool. I'm gonna call him now," he said. He pulled out his cell phone and started dialing numbers. I heard the phone ringing loudly from Jamie's phone. It took Ty-Ty seven rings before he answered the call.

"Yo, dude, what's up?" Ty-Ty greeted him.

"Hey, this is Jamie. The police just ran up on Eddie for that body near the spot, and I'm with the person who wants the job done. She wants me to help, since Ed is locked up. She said she feels comfortable that way," Jamie lied. I guess this was his way of securing a spot on the job, but in a passive-aggressive way.

"A'ight, I'm down with it. Just as long as the money don't change," Ty-Ty made it known.

"The only way the money is going to change is if you bring the other two with you. Ed is going to need some dough to get out, so I think we should drop one of your peoples."

Ty-Ty fell silent. At one point I thought that he was going to say no. But after mulling it over for a total of eighteen seconds he finally agreed to Jamie's terms.

"A'ight, let's do it," Ty-Ty said. "Meet us on Colonial Avenue at four o'clock," he added.

Jamie agreed and then they ended the call.

"How are you feeling about this? I mean, you're going into a war zone and you could run the risk of getting shot and killed," I expressed to him. Because what if something happened to him? His mother, Maggie, probably would not ever forgive me. And Eddie would find himself somewhere in the middle trying to defend me. And that is the last thing I wanted to happen.

"It ain't like I ain't already in the streets. I put my life on the line every day when I'm out with the other members of our gang. So, this right here ain't nothing but a walk in the park. Besides, I could use the money. Shit has been tight lately. Ed takes real good care of my mom, but I would like to do nice things for her too. Not only that, I really don't wanna live at my mom's crib, but every dollar I make in the streets go back in the streets. That's one of the rules in our gang. Whoever cashes in on a job, the old G's, like Ed,

Tommy Boy and a few more at the top of the food chain, they get paid first.

"Has this always been like this?"

"From day one."

"Well, don't worry, I'll hook you up on the side." I promised him.

25

POLICE HARASSMENT—UNCLE ED

I swear, what else bad could happen? Here I thought that I was going to be safe in the apartment if I didn't show my face, and got Jamie and Maggie to lie that I didn't live there—and nothing worked. Now here I was, sitting in the back of a police car and there was nothing I could do about it. I knew Maggie was going through it, because she didn't know how things would end with this situation.

"Didn't think that we were going to find you, huh?" the uniformed cop driving the squad car commented.

"Cracker, don't talk to me. You don't know shit about me!" I roared.

"I know that you killed an innocent guy just because he disrespected you," the cop continued.

"I didn't do shit. Whoever your source is, you need to get your money back."

"No, we got this information from the guy that the bullet was intended for," the cop in the passenger seat interjected.

"Yeah, a'ight. Whatever," I commented. I wasn't trying to hear what those two crackers were saying. That person that the bullet was intended for was dead. So I couldn't wait to see their faces when they found his dead body.

"Well, we're here," the driver announced.

I looked around the ground level of the garage that was connected to central booking. After they helped me out of the car, they escorted me inside the jail. They handed me off to this black correctional officer that I'm all too familiar with.

"Come on, Ed, I thought you said that you were never coming back," the CO reminded me.

I defended myself. "They got me on some bogus-ass shit. Talking about I killed somebody. I ain't did shit."

"I hope you're right," he replied, and then he and I walked towards a glass-encased holding room. There were about fifteen dudes and two women locked inside these two rooms that were side by side. Half the men looked like they were drug addicts and the other half looked like young boys that stole cars. I took a seat near the glass so I could see what was going on.

While I was fixated on everything going on outside this room, one of the young boys stepped up to me. "Ain't you an OG from the Ace of Spades?" I looked over my shoulder, and there standing behind me was a little dude that looked like he was barely sixteen years old. He looked gullible too. An old-timer would eat this little dude for breakfast and dinner and no one would help him.

"Yeah, young blood. What's your name?" I asked him, and then I turned around to give him my undivided attention.

"Monty," the young guy said proudly.

"Whatcha in here for?"

"They got me in here on a possession with intent to distribute a quarter pound of weed. I had that good shit too. But ain't you in here for that murder rap? Everybody on the street is talking about that shit. They said that you pumped lead in that dude Apple Head just because he disrespected you."

"Wherever you got that information from is wrong. Now get the fuck from around me because I will kill you with my bare hands," I warned the little dude.

"My bad!" the guy replied, and then he backed away from me.

I cannot believe that this little nigga walked up on me and tried to get some information from me. He just violated street code number two, *Keep your mouth closed while you're in jail.* I guess this dude didn't get the memo.

I sat in the holding room for four hours waiting on these motherfuckers to process me. And when I stood in front of the magistrate judge through a TV monitor, I was denied a bond. It was no surprise to me, because I know how this system works. This prison system is set up to keep dudes like me in jail. I just hope that it doesn't take long for these motherfuckers to let me go after they see that they don't have a witness for this case. Besides that, I knew Khloé was lost out there without me. I was the one that was supposed to orchestrate the hit, but now that I was in jail, I hoped that this didn't mess things up. I wished that I could call Maggie and give her instructions to notify Khloé and tell her to go to Tommy Boy. But I knew that I couldn't do it. All the phones in this jail, and every jail for that matter, are wired. You can't even send letters to the street with instructions or demands because the cops will intercept them, and then you're done. I could only hope that Khloé had enough sense to go to Tommy Boy on her own. *I guess I will find out sooner than later.*

26

PURE CHAOS—KHLOÉ

Instead of going to the spot to talk to Tommy Boy, Jamie and I decided to meet Ty-Ty at four o'clock. It was a little after two, so I got Jamie to ride with me to Frances's house. I needed to make sure that there wasn't going to be any funny business when this mission went down. He was shocked at what I was going to do. He even laughed. "Yo, this is funny. I have never been on a stakeout before. This is the shit that cops do."

"Yes, it is. But I've got a lot riding on this, so I need to make sure that nothing changes. Also, my uncle's get-out-of-jail-free card is on the line too," I told him.

"I can respect that," Jamie said as we headed in the direction of Frances's house.

I wasn't sure if she'd be home when I got there, and thankfully she was. And what was even greater was that Ryan was there too. I got two birds with one stone. How beautiful was that? Immediately after I parked my car, I pulled out my device and aimed in the direction of Frances's house. Jamie just sat beside me in awe.

The first five minutes of the transmission was Frances and Ryan having sex. Jamie found this so amusing. "Damn, it sounds like he's fucking the shit out of her," he commented.

I cracked a smile because I agreed.

"This shit here is better than watching a reality show," he added. And then he chuckled.

"Shhhhhh, bring it down some."

"What . . . Can they hear me?"

"No, they can't. But I am trying to hear them," I told him.

"My bad," he said, and then he fell silent.

As soon as the escapade was over, Frances started talking about the hit for today. "Think our plan is going to work?" She started off the conversation.

"Oh, 'course it is. All I gotta do is let them go in first. They get whacked, I shoot off a couple of rounds into the wall or floor to make it look like I was firing back, and then that's it," he explained.

Jamie looked at me. "So, this cop is setting up his cop buddies?" he whispered to me.

I nodded my head.

"Yo, these crackers are grimy."

"Yes, they are," I agreed.

"Don't forget that while I'm at the precinct making my report that you already have the van. We've gotta be on time for this load. You know they are sticklers for time."

"Of course I know. I'm the one that set up this whole operation from the beginning."

Ryan didn't comment on Frances's statement. He changed the direction of the conversation. "Can you believe it? We're gonna make a million and a half for this shipment. And all we gotta do is give Nick his part, and that's it."

"Don't forget that news reporter's uncle. We still owe him money."

"That's nothing. He doesn't count. That's chump change."

I looked at Jamie. "Chump change, huh?" I commented.

"I guess he's right, they are getting a million and a half," he replied.

"It sounds like they're picking up a lot of drugs," I mentioned.

"Yeah, it does. And I know one thing. I sure would like to get my hands on it," Jamie said, and he rubbed his hands together.

"No, they can keep that. I just want to get what they owe and get my uncle out of jail."

"Speak for yourself, 'cause that million and a half sounds way better now that I think about it."

"You never told me how you got Brad and Chris to agree to go to that house on Lexington to do a drug bust," we heard Frances say.

"I told all of them that one of my confidant informers told me that a new group of guys from New York just opened shop in that house, and they make twenty-five thousand dollars a day selling heroin. And they just got a shipment last night, so today would be a good day to run in there," Ryan explained.

"Just be careful, baby. You know that me and our bundle of joy needs you."

Jamie and I heard them kiss. "Yes, I know," he assured her.

"Too bad that Gavin ain't here to get in on this action. If he would've kept his mouth closed about going to Internal Affairs, he would've been three hundred and fifty thousand dollars richer."

"Ryan, it wasn't just Internal Affairs, remember he found out about our relationship and that I was pregnant, and that's why he wanted to shut our operation down."

"Well, I bet he wished that he would've done differently.

Look at us, we're living the life, baby. We got the money from the last shipment, we got the money coming from this shipment, we got our baby, we got each other, and we're gonna live like we're on vacation for the rest of our lives," Ryan bragged.

"Sounds good to me," she commented, and before another word was exchanged, someone's cell phone rang.

"Hello," I heard Ryan say.

"Hey, dude, Brad wants to know what time is that bust?" I heard an unfamiliar voice say.

"Chris, it's at four thirty."

"Are we just taking their currency and product? Or are we locking them up?"

"I was thinking since we had that job later on, why don't we just run in and out," Ryan insisted.

"Sounds good. Sounds good. Are we on course for later? You know we gotta be on time because the last time was a disaster. That one Russian guy got in Brad's face and we can't have that anymore. We don't wanna get into another brawl with those guys. Because I don't think we'll be able to hold Brad back this time around," Chris explained.

"Yeah, I know. We can't have that happen again," Ryan agreed.

"Okay. So, we're all riding in the same car?"

"Yes, we are. So, I'll meet you guys in our usual spot."

"Done," Chris replied.

After Ryan ended his call with Chris, Jamie and I sat back and looked at one another. "Yo, those crackers are dirty as fuck! They do dudes in the street foul and then they turn around and do the same shit to their partners," Jamie commented.

"I know. It's crazy," I added. Ryan and Frances talked more but it wasn't anything to call home about. So, while

Jamie and I sat outside Frances's house, we saw Ryan leave, one of her neighbors walk their dog, the city garbage truck driver come through to collect trash, as well a group of landscapers manicuring a nearby neighbor's lawn. Through it all, I got a moment to talk to Jamie. "When we talked earlier, you said that Ed takes care of your mother and how you appreciate that. So, how is your personal relationship with my uncle?" I started off asking him.

"It's been cool. But we've had our off days."

"Has he ever argued with your mother around you?"

"A couple of times. But it's never got to the point that they said they wanna break up."

"Have you ever heard him call her a bitch or hoe?"

"Hell nah, he knows better."

"So, how long have you been in the Ace of Spades?"

"Since I was fifteen."

"How old are you now?"

"I'm twenty."

"Is your father in your life?"

"Nope, he got shot and killed when I was like six going on seven years old."

"How does it feel not having your father in your life?"

"Sometimes I get mad because if I wanna talk about something that only my dad could give me good advice on, he's not here to do it. Father's Day messes me up too. Especially when I see other dudes hanging out with their fathers."

"Do you look at Eddie as a father figure?"

"Nah, my relationship with him is like a big brother type."

"Do you have a grandmother or aunts and uncles on your father's side of the family?"

"My grandmother is dead. She died of old age. My grandfather is dead too. I do have two aunts that live not too far from where my mom and I live. I'm not close to them though."

"What about cousins?"

"Both of my aunts got kids. But they're all girls. And they're young, like from ten years old to thirteen."

"Am I asking too many questions?" I asked him and cracked a smile.

"Nah, you're cool. It's not that often when I can talk to someone that's smart. All the people I be around say stupid shit all the time."

"Well, that's refreshing to know. So, did you graduate from high school?"

"Nah, I am going back to get my GED, though."

"What was the last grade you finished?"

"I dropped out of school while I was in the eighth grade."

"Why?"

"Because I wouldn't get up and go to school. I would hang out all night with my homeboys and when the morning came I'd be too tired to go."

"Where are those guys now?"

"One of them is dead."

"How?"

"Got shot and killed by one of our rival gangs. And the other two guys is locked up. One in juvie and the other one is locked up in the county."

"Have you ever been locked up?"

"Yeah, but it was stupid. And I only did sixty days."

"What did you do?"

"The cops was fucking with me because I was smoking weed on the corner at one of the corner stores. I think the guy that owns the store called on us. Oh yeah, they gave me two years of probation too. My probation officer showed up at my mom's house yesterday talking about she came to give me a piss test and she didn't even do it. She walked out of my house without giving me a test. But she searched the house. Well, she didn't get to search my mom's bedroom because the door was locked. Ed was hiding in the closet."

"Has she ever done that before?"

"Nah, she'll make sure that I still live there by checking my room for boy things, like my clothes and stuff. She'll ask me questions and then she'll make me give her a piss test, but this time she didn't. So I know the cops sent her in there."

"Where were you when the cops kicked in your mother's front door?"

"We were in the kitchen talking. And as soon as they saw us, they told us to get down on the floor. It was like they knew that he was in the house, even though he hadn't shown his face on the streets since that thing happened. My mom thinks that maybe our neighbor Lily had something to do with the cops showing up."

"Why is that?"

"Because yesterday two cops ran up on me while I was taking trash to the dumpster. They wanted to know my name. Where I lived. Then they asked me if I knew Ed and where he was. But I wasn't giving them crackers no play. So, they handcuffed me and made me sit on the curb. And while they had me sitting on the curb, I was talking more shit to them and I was pissing them off too. They ended up letting me go after my moms came downstairs raising hell."

"I'm sure that was unfortunate."

"For them it was. 'Cause see, I don't give a damn about those cops, especially when I know that I'm straight. I don't have any pending charges hanging over my head, I don't carry drugs on me, and I don't have a burner. So I'm good. And they hate it."

"You better be careful. I see all of these cops are killing young guys such as yourself."

"Yeah, I see it all the time on social media, but I'm good. I know how to outsmart them."

I let out a long sigh. It was apparent that this little guy thought that he had the whole world figured out. So I left well enough alone.

27

ORANGE IS THE NEW BLACK—UNCLE ED

They got me in cell block two with a bunch of young dudes. Thank God there were also a couple of my gang members in the same cell block as me. Fat Man, G-Money, Prince, L-Wood, and Dee all greeted me as soon as I walked inside the unit. There were five men in total, so I knew my safety wouldn't be an issue. I gave each one of them the hand to back pat, and then they escorted me to the room I would be sharing with one of them. "Yo, dude, what's good?" Dee asked me. He was the oldest among us, so he was the leader. I was also his cell mate.

"I ain't doing so good right now. Gotta fight these charges," I replied.

"Yeah, we heard about that. Elroy caught a dope charge, so he came through a few days ago. His girl bonded him out though."

"Dee, man, that nigga disrespected me in front of a new member. So, you know I couldn't have that shit. I had to make an example out of him."

"Yeah, I hear you. You did the right thing. But the thing

that I am interested in knowing is, did you take care of the dude that ran off?" Dee's questions continued, while the other four men stood around like they were bodyguards.

"Oh, most definitely. I got him eliminated yesterday. He's a done deal."

"Well, then you ain't gonna have no problems, especially when those crackers find out they ain't got no witness."

"Exactly," I agreed.

"So, how is business out there? Are we bringing in any money?" Dee wanted to know.

Dee was a high-ranking soldier like Tommy Boy, and each one of them had a spot. And when money was made, it was divided up amongst the leaders. The rest of it went to the workers that brought the money in. So, I was thinking that he was talking about this drug bust hit on the cops later. I couldn't quite see where this conversation was going, but I knew that I needed to be straight-up with him or he was gonna have me stabbed, and oust my ass immediately thereafter.

"We've been working on the things that may come through tonight or tomorrow," I finally said, making sure I used my words correctly.

"How much are we looking at?"

"Twenty to thirty grand, if not more."

"Oh, that's a nice payday," Dee commented.

"Yeah, it sho' is," Fat Man and Prince replied simultaneously.

"If the cops hadn't ran up in my crib, I would be out there making moves and I'd know exactly how much was coming."

"Who's out there working on it while you're in here?"

I hesitated for a moment, trying to decide whether I should involve my niece. This nigga I was talking to right now wasn't nothing to play with. He would kill his mother if she stole one hundred dollars from him. So I needed to be very careful with the words I used. "I spoke to Ty-Ty and he's gonna handle things."

"Does Tommy Boy know about it?"

"Yep. I talked to him first. He's the one that appointed Ty-Ty to do the job."

"What kind of job is it?"

Now here I go, once again in a situation that involved my niece. But I refused to say her name, and especially to this madman. "You know about those dirty-ass narc cops that be taking niggas' packages and money and don't arrest them?" I started off saying, "Well, the lady of the dead cop that they said killed himself, found out that his partners killed him and made it look like a suicide. So now that she knows this, she wants to set them up to get killed."

"How much is she paying?"

"See, that's the thing, we were still negotiating that. I was waiting for her to call me back, but this bullshit happened."

"A'ight, don't worry, I'll make sure it gets done," he assured me. But I didn't need him to get involved. Tommy Boy and I got this deal on lock. The money was already going through a lot of hands now. We didn't need any more.

28

LET THE GAMES BEGIN—KHLOÉ

Jamie and I exchanged cell phone numbers and then I dropped Jamie off at three forty-five, a block from the house on Lexington Avenue. I circled around the neighborhood twice, looking for a good spot to park my car. I needed a place where I wouldn't be seen but close enough where I could use my satellite listening device. Unfortunately, I could not find one. I did, however, find Frances's car parked four cars ahead of me on this one-way street, so I pulled over curbside and watched her. She was in her car alone, so I figured that she was there because she wanted to see the show that was about to go down.

While I was sitting in the car waiting for the great finale, I got a call from Jamie. "Hello," I answered.

"Ty-Ty and them ain't here yet, so I've got a few minutes to talk."

"Do you think that this is the right time to talk?" I asked him. What if one of this gang's members came in the house while he was on the phone with me?

"Yeah, we good. Dem dudes don't tell me what to do."

"I just want you to be careful."

"I told you that I'm good."

"Well, since you're good, I want you to know that the dead cop's wife is outside watching the house."

"How long has she been there?"

"She had to have just pulled up, because I rode down this one-way street twice before, and on this third run, I saw her car parked on the right side of the street," I explained, and then my thoughts shifted to the back of the house. "Oh no, Jamie, I just saw those dirty-ass cops run up to the back of the house. Where are you?" I said nervously.

"I'm downstairs near the kitchen."

"Do you have any drugs or guns on you?"

"I don't have no drugs on me, but I got my burner."

"You need to find a place to hide, or they will take your gun and lock you up."

"I thought that they wasn't coming until four thirty."

I know, me too. But let's not talk about it. Go and hide somewhere."

"Okay, I'm going upstairs in the attic."

"Is it one of those attics that has a pull-down ladder?"

"Yeah, I'm pulling it down now."

"Hurry up, because they're looking through the back and side windows to see if someone is inside," I warned him.

"I'm pulling the door closed now," he told me.

"When they come in the house, make sure you don't make a sound."

"But what about my soldiers? They supposed to be here in a minute."

"You can't worry about them right now. You gotta worry about you. You're the one in the hot seat."

"Hey wait, I hear them coming through the back door," he whispered.

"Okay, put me on mute but don't hang up. Because I wanna hear everything they say."

"I'm doing it now."

I sat there in my car and listened to Brad and the other cops as they tore the house up looking for guns and drugs. Brad and Chris didn't like the idea of being there and not getting any action. "I thought you said that there's gonna be a lot of thugs in here with money and drugs?" Brad said.

"My CI told me that they were going to be here by four thirty. And I told you that," I heard Ryan say.

"Yeah, Brad, I'm with you. This was a hoax."

After Chris made his comment, I ended my call with Jamie, but then I saw three guys walking up to the back of the same house. I had to text Jamie and let him know that his boys were about to walk through the back door. He didn't respond, so I became worried. More fearful to be exact. But then I remembered that I could power on my satellite device and aim it at Frances's car just in case she had a few words to say.

For the first twenty-five seconds I didn't hear her say anything. But then I heard her voice. "The guys are coming through the back door, so let's get in position. We can't screw this up," Frances said.

"Okay," Ryan replied, and then the call ended.

From the looks of it and the body language of Ty-Ty, he must've gotten Jamie's text because he and the other guys backed off from going in the back door and decided to climb in the house from the side window. I watched Ty-Ty and his boys while also keeping an eye on Frances, making sure she stayed in her lane.

After the last guy climbed in through the window, I immediately started hearing gunshots. *Boom! Boom! Boom! Pop! Pop! Pop!* I heard at least twenty-five to thirty-five gunshots. My heart sank to the pit of my stomach. My heart rate picked up too. I didn't know whether to drive away or wait here and see what happened. I hoped Jamie was all right. I knew something like this was going to go down, but to actually hear it took it to another level.

Because of all the chaos, I didn't realize that I still had the satellite on Frances until she started talking again. "Come on, Ryan, come out of there, baby," she whispered. I could hear the crackling sound in her voice. It sounded like she was crying or about to cry. "Come on, baby, please come out of there," she whimpered.

A few minutes later, Ty-Ty and the other three guys fled the scene. They scattered off in three different directions. A couple seconds after that, Ryan ran out of the front door and cued Frances to leave, and then he went back inside the house. The only person that didn't come outside was Jamie. So, I texted him. Where are you? Are you still in the attic? But I got no response. So I sat there, knowing that I shouldn't be there. In the distance, I heard paramedics, police cruisers, and fire trucks heading in my direction, but that didn't put any pressure on me to leave. And while I mulled over whether or not I should leave, I saw Ryan come back out the house. This time he headed to my car. When he got within four feet of my car he held his hands out, and there, sitting in the palm of his hand, was Jamie's Canabus printed cell phone. My heart leaped from my chest.

"What is this?" I asked him. But I knew what it was and who it belonged to.

"The young guy that was hiding ETA this is it right here what's up that is it is all last night it's just like the flu drawls what's this yeah call me what what's this close hey says it he is still holding pause it virus in the attic. I didn't want my other colleagues to find it and then implicate you in this shooting," Ryan said.

I took Jamie's cell phone from his hand. "So, everyone in there is dead?" I asked him.

"Yes, they are."

"I thought that you were supposed to spare Nick's life."

"I tried to, but he got in the line of fire," Ryan said, and then he smiled. It was one of those wicked smiles too.

"What about the one you took this cell phone from? How did he get caught in the line of fire?"

"No one knew that he was hiding in the attic. All he had to do was stay quiet. But no, he wanted to play hero and started unloading his gun from the door in the attic. I didn't kill him, though."

"Well, who did it?"

"Chris got him before one of those other guys unloaded their ammo on Chris."

"Why did y'all go so early? You know that the job was supposed to happen at four thirty."

"I know. I tried telling that to Brad, but he didn't wanna listen. I may be wrong, but I have a hunch that he may have known that it was a setup. Think someone could've done that?" Ryan said in an insinuating manner.

"Why are you looking at me like that? I don't know him personally, so you can cancel any thought that may be the opposite of mine. As a matter of fact, I can't stand the sick fuck! Raping women by making them suck his dick and stealing from drug dealers. All of you cops give all the other cops a bad rep."

"Not me. I'm a good guy."

"Don't come at me with that bullshit! I know what you are all about. Sleeping with Gavin's wife. And I know that's your baby she's carrying too."

Ryan displayed another wicked grin. "Who told you that?" he wanted to know.

"I've got my sources just like you have yours," I told him in a matter-of-fact manner.

Ryan's attention shifted when he saw the paramedics approaching us. "Gotta go. And you should be too," he said, and then he walked back to the house.

When I realized that I wouldn't be able to get out of there for another hour or so if I got blocked in by the first responders, I took Ryan's advice and left. While I was driving away, I tried to grapple with the fact that Jamie was dead. Now how was I going to tell Maggie? She was going to hate me. And she might even attack me. Damn! I wished that I had left Jamie home with her. I knew I was going to feel guilty about this for the rest of my life.

I really wanted to just take my ass home, but I had to finish this job. I couldn't let Frances get away with the rest of the money that she owed my uncle Eddie and now Maggie. It was Ryan's duty to bring Brad and the rest of those losers to the house at 4:45, not 3:55. *I don't care how she sees it. She owes us a great deal and I'm gonna make sure that she pays her debt.*

Once I had gotten away from all the commotion of the blaring horns and sirens, I grabbed my cell phone and dialed her number. She surprised me when she answered my call on the second ring. "I've been waiting on your call," she said.

"You didn't have to wait on my call. You could've called me first," I let her know.

"I don't like to rush things," she said calmly.

"Look, Frances, cut the crap. Meet me so I can get the rest of the money," I snapped. She was playing too many mind games at this point, and I wasn't in the mood. Especially now that Jamie was dead.

"Where do you wanna meet?"

"Let's meet at the Royal Farms service station near my house," Frances suggested.

"I will be there, and I want you to bring me my money, my uncle's money, and the money for my uncle's stepson who got caught up in the crossfire. His mother needs some life insurance!" I roared through the phone.

"It's not my fault that he was killed. Take that up with your uncle. He's the one that sent him into the line of fire."

"Frances, say something else that I don't like and I will drop dime on all of you."

"Well, when you do, just know that your uncle will spend the rest of his life in prison and you will receive a thirty-year sentence on a murder-for-hire charge."

"Is that a threat?" I asked her, seething.

"No, it's not a threat. It's a promise," she insisted, refusing to back down.

I sucked my teeth. "What time are we meeting?" I asked her.

"Give me two hours and I will be there," she replied. And before she could utter another word, I disconnected our call.

Instead of waiting for Frances to meet me at the service station, I headed over to her house because I knew she was there. According to her earlier plans, she was going to get things together while at home, and once the trade-off happened, she and Ryan would go off into the sunset. So my best bet was to go and monitor her movements to find out what was in this shipment that she and Ryan had talked about.

While en route to Frances's house, my cell phone started ringing. But when I looked down, I realized that it wasn't my cell phone that was ringing. In fact, it was Jamie's cell phone. I picked it up from the cup holder in my car and looked at the caller ID. It was Maggie calling. I started to answer it but I couldn't bring myself to do it. What was I going to say when she answered? Tell her that Jamie was dead? Tell her that I took him to his death? I swear, it would just break my heart if I had to do that.

Thankfully, his cell phone stopped ringing. Because if I would've heard one more ring, I would've powered his cell phone off.

Hearing it ring fueled guilt inside of me that I had led Jamie to his death. I only wished that my uncle Eddie was on the streets. He would've taken care of all this.

Once again I found myself cruising down Frances's street

so that I could stake out her home and find out what else she had up her sleeve. This shipment that she was prepping for was number-one on her priority list, so I needed to be front and center. Immediately after I parked my car, I aimed my satellite disk at her house and got a hit.

"What do you mean, he left?" I heard Frances say. I could tell that she and Ryan had been on the phone for a few minutes before I zeroed in on their conversation with him talking through her speakerphone.

"When I went out to the car to give that bitch the cell phone that belonged to the thug that was hiding in the attic, I went back inside the house, and he was gone. I knew he was hit because he left a trail of blood drops as he walked out the back door," Ryan explained.

"So, what are we going to do?" Frances asked. She seemed worried.

"We're gonna keep going as planned, because for all we know, he could be lying in the ditch dead somewhere because I shot him too. He got hit with at least five rounds."

"You better hope so, because I don't want any screwups. Oh, and I spoke to the fake-ass news reporter and she told me that a guy died in the house. It was her uncle's girl-friend's son."

"When did you talk to her?"

"I talked to her about twenty-five minutes ago.
She wants retribution for him."

"Fuck that! They only get what was promised, and that's it."

"I don't even want to give her that. I say, let's keep the other portion of it. I mean, it's not like she can go to the cops and tell them that I paid her and her uncle to pull off a job. Who do you think they will believe?"

"Well, if you feel like that, we might as well let her uncle rot in jail."

"I think so too. It'll be easy to get one of my confidant informers to say that they saw him pull the trigger, since both of the victims are dead and won't be able to testify."

"Let's get the ball rolling, then. I mean, to be honest we really don't have time to fix his situation anyway. . . . We gotta get the van, take care of the kids, and once we get the money, we could head out of here."

"I love it when a plan comes together," he commented.

"You do know that Khloé knows about us?"

"What do you mean *us*?"

"When I handed her the boy's cell phone, she told me that she knew that you and I are having an affair and she knows that the baby in your belly is mine."

"Are you freaking serious?" Frances seemed taken aback. "How did she know that?"

"I don't know. So we have to keep her happy as long as we can and until we leave."

"Are you at the precinct yet?"

"I just got here."

"What if Brad shows up?"

"Frances, he's not going to show up. He's dead. After the guys shot him, I put a couple of rounds in him too."

"What about the other cops?"

"What about them? I didn't have to do anything to them. The gang members took care of him. Before I left the scene, I watched the coroners take all the bodies out. Chris, Nick and the young guy."

"How do you feel?"

"I feel good. I gave a statement at the scene, and now I'm down at the precinct giving them a more thorough statement and when I'm done with that, I'm gonna come straight to you so we can get the van. And from there, we go by the shelter, pick up all twenty kids, and deliver them to the highest bidder."

"You know that we can get at least one hundred thousand

dollars per kid? Because remember the last time we fucked up because we were so anxious to get the money and go. Now we know what we have, so we will go in there with our thinking caps on and get this money." Frances continued, saying, "Think we could get more children? Isabella said that we could have as many kids as we could take. Shit, instead of renting a van, we could get a bus. I mean, it's not like the mothers are going to come around looking for their kids. Remember, we're sitting on a gold mine."

"Yeah, I know. But we've gotta be careful and not be greedy. Twenty kids is plenty. Let's just maximize them," he pointed out. Even though he was a piece of shit, he did have some sense.

"I'm so glad that Gavin isn't in the picture anymore. He tried to block us from doing another one of these jobs. If he only would've stayed with the program. But no, he wanted to have a heart after seeing that one little girl crying. How old was she? Eleven?"

"I think so."

"Talking about letting her go, after the little girl said that she'd been raped by her uncles, and all she wanted was to live like a little kid." I heard Frances mimic the little girl. From the sound of this recollection, that little girl cried to those fucking bums because all she wanted to do was be a normal kid again. But this bitch was making a mockery out of that situation. I swear, if I could sell her into human trafficking, I would in a heartbeat.

"So, have you done everything?"

"Yes, I've already packed everything we need."

"What about the money?"

"I got that too. When I had Khloé follow me to the bank, I pulled out all the money we had in the safety deposit box."

"Good girl!"

"I love you."

"I love you, too. See you soon."

Enraged, what I just heard made me sick to my stomach. This was the shipment they were talking about? *They're into human trafficking? They sell innocent little kids? How fucking revolting is that? This bitch is pregnant herself and has the nerve to sell children to rich pedophiles? On top of that, this isn't her first time doing it. Now it makes sense, about her dead husband wanting to rat them out. That's why they killed him and made it look like a suicide. These fucking monsters. But I'll tell you one thing, they won't get away with this.*

29

I CAN'T TAKE THIS RIGHT NOW— UNCLE ED

Since I hadn't been able to start a phone account at the jail, I got my homeboy G-Money to call my crib so I could talk to Maggie and see what's been going on since I've been in this hellhole.

"Hey, baby, you know it's crazy because I've only been in here for a couple hours and I miss you already," I started off saying.

"Ed, the police just killed my baby," Maggie said softly, and then she started crying.

"*The police did what?*" I roared through the phone.

"They shot and killed Jamie. They killed him in a house on Lexington Avenue," she replied. Her words became more and more piercing.

"What happened, OG?" G-Money seemed concerned.

"The motherfucking cops murdered Jamie. My wife's son," I told him. When I heard the words coming out of my mouth, it broke my heart. All Maggie had was Jamie. He was her life and now he was gone. But what's worse was that I was not out there to support her. And getting those motherfucking cops that did it. "How did you find out?" I asked her.

"A couple of the guys that hang with him told me. I'm on my way over to that house now."

"You're in the car driving?"

"Yes," she said as she continued to sob.

"Damn, baby, I hate hearing you like that. Fuck! I'm supposed to be home when this type of shit happens!" I snapped. I couldn't hold my sanity anymore. "Did Jamie's boys say anything else besides the cops killing hm?"

"Yes, they said three cops are dead too. It was a drug bust that went to the left."

"Have you talked to my niece?" I asked her. I didn't want to say her name because I knew that these phones were recorded.

"Not since she and Jamie left a couple hours ago. He was supposed to take her to see Tommy Boy, so now I'm trying to figure out how he ended up at the house on Lexington. Did she take him there or what?" Maggie explained, and in my opinion she was talking too much. I wished I could tell her to shut her mouth. All I asked was have you seen her? That's it. I didn't ask her to say her name on this heavily recorded line.

"I'll tell you what, go out there and find out what you can and I'll call you later."

"Hey, wait, did they give you a bond? Because right now, I need you out here with me." Her sobs got louder.

"No, I didn't get one. But I'm gonna work something out. Trust me," I assured her. As badly as I wanted to tell her that because that hit job on those cops was completed, I was gonna be given a pass to get out of jail, I couldn't. It was okay, though, because I was gonna be home with her sooner than she thought.

"I love you."

"I love you too, baby," I told her.

I was enraged while talking to Maggie because now I knew that Khloé brought him in to help with that job. And where was she? Maggie just said that three cops were dead, so what happened? And what three cops were killed? Not being able to get those answers right now was making me annoyed on all levels. I hated being in the dark. This shit was driving me fucking insane.

"What's going on? I heard you saying that your wife's son is dead?" OG Dee asked me after I walked into our cell.

I rubbed both of my hands across my head. "Yeah, he was a part of that job that I was telling you about. She said that he died, and three cops."

"Narcs?" Dee asked. He wanted clarity.

"Yeah, three of the cops that be taking dudes' drugs and money."

"So how did it happen?"

"I can't really say. You know we gotta be careful about what we say on those fucking phones."

"Oh yeah, you're right."

"Damn, I hated hearing her cry like she was doing. That shit was fucking me up inside."

"I'm sorry for your loss. But you gotta look at things like this: Even though we lost one, the other side lost three. So we came out on top," he said. And even though what he was saying was true, I didn't want to hear another dude talk about Jamie like that. He was talking like that kid wasn't indispensable and that was not cool. If Maggie would've heard Dee say that shit around her, there was no doubt in my mind that she would've cursed that nigga out and probably would've swung on him with that bat we had in the hall closet. And then that's when I would step in and defend my woman.

Sitting in jail with my hands tied, I got a seat in the TV room so I could gather my thoughts. I also started watching TV just in case I could catch the latest news. I already knew about Jamie's fate, now I need to check on my niece.

30

KIDS' LIVES MATTER—KHLOÉ

I felt sick to my stomach after hearing Ryan and that bitch talk about how much they could make, trafficking innocent children. I mean, this bitch was pregnant. She had a baby inside of her, so how could she be so insensitive about someone else's children? *This bitch is a greedy monster and I'm gonna make sure that she doesn't get away with this.*

Thinking about how this whore didn't plan on helping my uncle get out of jail and pay the remaining balance for that job, I sat in my car, wanting so badly to bring down my wrath. I could do so many things to this bitch, whether she knew it or not. I guess she felt like since I was a retired journalist that I didn't have any spunk or rage inside of me. *I will show her.*

I started sifting through the documents that Frances gave me when I started investigating the cops. I searched the first page with Brad's information on it and located his cell phone number. After I found it, I grabbed my cell phone, blocked my cell phone number, and called it. I knew that it might be a long shot that he'd answer it, since Ryan said that Brad wasn't in the house when he went back in. But I tested it anyway. His cell phone rang seven times and then it stopped. "Fuck!" I pouted. "Damn, Brad, where are you? Dead in a ditch or what?" I whispered.

I waited five minutes and then I called his cell phone number again. It rang six times this time and no answer. I sighed heavily and wondered if I was pressing my luck with this one. Now I figured since I knew that Frances wasn't going to pay the rest of the money she owed and that her plans were to go and pick up a van and then take a large group of kids to pedophiles who happened to be rich, I knew I had an edge over her. I would confront her.

Talk about being restless. I was so tired of sitting in my car and keeping a watch on Frances, I almost called her to pick her brain the same way I did Ryan. I wanted to hear her tone when I told her that I knew everything about her ass. But I decided against it. She wasn't gonna be straight-up with me anyway, so why bother. I did, however, dial Brad's number again. I figured what the hell. It's not like I was gonna lose anything. So when I called him this third time, the phone rang four times and then I heard dead air. Someone answered and didn't utter one word. I was afraid to say hello, for fear of another cop finding it and asking about my involvement with Brad. Well, I guess I could say that I met him at the dinner party the other night? And now realizing that I could probably get away with it, I finally said, "Hello," but my tone was very low. It was almost a whisper.

"Brad, is this you?" I asked.

"Who is this?" Brad asked me.

"This is Khloé, the TV journalist you met at the Gomez's dinner party," I explained.

"What do you want?" His questions continued.

"I wanna help you. I know about what happened back at that house on Lexington. And I know who set you up," I began to tell him. Despite the fact that he was a cold-hearted rapist, I figured why not start a war with he, Ryan and Frances? Let them kill each other if they chose to do.

"What house? What are you talking about?" I could sense that he was very leery of me.

"Brad, now I don't agree with how you treat drug dealers in the streets, but at the same time, I don't think it's fair to take another person's life. Frances and Ryan set you up. The shipment that's gonna be auctioned off later tonight, well, they wanted to keep all the money. That's why those black guys were there. They were paid to kill you, Chris, and Nick."

"How the fuck do you know all of this?"

"Because that's what I do. I find out shit."

"So what do you want from me?"

"I wanna help you get revenge."

"Why is that?"

"Because I like your wife and she needs her husband."

"You're not trying to set me up, are you?"

"No, I am not. And so you know, Frances is at her house right now, packing her and Ryan's stuff so immediately after the kids are bought, they're gonna leave town."

"Fucking bitch! I knew she was a cunt when Gavin first introduced all of us to her. He really loved that girl, but she wanted something more."

"Yes, I know."

"Well, do you know that she set him up to be killed? He didn't commit suicide. When he told her that he was leaving her after finding out about the baby, and that he was closing down this operation, she went stone-cold crazy. I don't know what that girl got going on down in her private area, but whatever it is, it's got those guys going crazy over her."

"Do you wanna get revenge?"

"You fucking right I do. But I'm hurt. That motherfucker

Ryan shot me once in the fucking stomach. I've lost a lot of blood."

"Where are you? I can come and get you."

"No, I'm fine."

"Listen, Brad, I can come and get you. Don't you want to confront Ryan and Frances? You can't let them get away with this," I begged him. I wanted to see Frances's ass buried underneath the jail.

"All right, well, I'll tell you what. I'm gonna have my wife come and get me and then I'll meet you at the warehouse next to an old elementary school on South Street at eleven o'clock."

"Are you gonna really come?" I asked him, because he was making it too easy to be turned in to the cops.

"Yes, I will be there. I've gotta make a lot of things right for people that I've done wrong."

"Okay, I'll see you at eleven."

I couldn't believe what I just heard come out of Brad's mouth. Finally I heard someone taking responsibility for the shit they'd done wrong and wanted to correct it. Immediately after I ended the call with Brad, I grabbed my cell phone and made an important call.

"Hey Ginger, you got time to talk?"

It seemed like the hours were going by extremely slow. But nevertheless, the time came and it was time to take action. Brad had me meet him at the warehouse next to the old elementary school, so I beat him there. I don't like being in the blind. I saw that firsthand when the shootout went down at the house on Lexington. I also had a friend meet me there too. Brad, on the other hand, came in a few minutes after my friend did. He announced his presence as soon as he parked his car. I thought that he was going to bring his wife, but I guess those plans changed. We all sat there in our cars and waited for the action to begin. And the action is what we got, after a black van drove slowly into the warehouse. And then another black van slowly rolled in. Two more dark-colored vans drove into the warehouse. In all, I saw a total of four vans. One by one, everyone started exiting their vans. It was something that you'd see on TV.

I texted my friend, who was also filming with her cell-phone. Are you seeing this?

Yes, I am, she replied.

Oh my God! They just brought out the first child. It looks like a little girl.

I know. I see her too.

I texted her again. He's holding her in his arms like she's drugged up or something. Contact your person now.

She texted back. I'm already on it.

Before I could blink my eyes, sirens started blaring loudly. I knew I saw at least a dozen squad cars and five undercover cars rushing into the warehouse. I watched Frances from where I was and she tried her best to run away, but one of the cops grabbed her. I watched the white men that came to bid on those kids get rounded up too. After everyone was appre-hended, my friend from the news station walked over to the crime scene. Brad got out of his car too. I could tell that he was fixed up a bit, but he was still leaking blood. A couple of his cop buddies saw how weak he was and grabbed him by the arms. If they hadn't, he would've fallen to the ground.

"Brad, you're alive!" Ryan yelled towards him.

Ginger asked her cameraman to turn the camera towards Ryan, but I got the cameraman to put the camera back on Brad. "Don't listen to that fraud over there. Listen to him," I said as I watched Brad stand there in agony. I almost began to feel sorry for him.

"I'm here to set the record straight since my time is running out. I was shot earlier by my partner over there," Brad started off and pointed towards Ryan.

"That's a fucking lie! Don't believe him!" Ryan snapped.

"Me and my other officers were set up to be killed by him. We were at that house on Lexington to be ambushed and killed by some young thugs that he and Frances Larson paid."

"That's a lie and you know it!" Frances yelled.

"We are here tonight because of a human trafficking scheme we started," he continued, and then he started choking. I could tell that he was on his last legs. It seemed like at any minute he was going to die.

"Hold him up," I heard another cop say.

"Are you saying all of this to make peace with yourself?" Ginger asked him.

"Yes, I am. I was a bad, bad man. And I have done some bad things to people, and I've got to make things right by apologizing to everyone."

Ginger pressed him. "What about your partner in crime refuting everything you're saying? He's denying everything."

"Check my journal at my house. I've got everything in there. What I've done and who I've done it to. I've got to make things right with God before I leave this earth," he continued.

Brad told everything under the sun. He didn't leave anything out. A few minutes after they called paramedics, Brad passed. Everyone stood there in awe. "Did you get that shot?" Ginger asked her camera guy.

"Yep, I got it," he replied.

"Come on, let's go over here to the other cop and his mistress," Ginger instructed him.

As soon as she approached, Frances snapped, "Get the fuck away from me!"

I stood on the sidelines laughing at her silly ass. I knew that she regretted hiring me to be her private investigator.

She must've seen me smiling because she took her anger up another notch. "Do you think that I'm going down by myself? You accepted dirty money from me so you're going to jail too. I'm gonna tell them everything!" I heard her yell while I headed back to my car.

I covered my tracks from the day she hired me to investigate her husband's murder. So, I'm in the clear and there's nothing she can do about it.

Who's the dumb bitch now?

Missed how Khloé got her start?
Be sure to read
THE DEADLINE
Available now

MAY - - 2021